HARLEQUIN®
Presents~

Welcome to February's fabulous collection of books from Harlequin Presents!

Be sure not to miss the final installment of the brilliant series THE ROYAL HOUSE OF NIROLI. Will the beautiful island of Niroli finally be able to crown the true heir to the throne? Find out in *A Royal Bride at the Sheikh's Command* by favorite author Penny Jordan! Plus, continuing her trilogy about three passionate and brooding men, THE RICH, THE RUTHLESS AND THE REALLY HANDSOME, Lynne Graham brings you *The Greek Tycoon's Defiant Bride,* where Leonidas is determined to take the mother of his son as his wife!

Also this month…can a billionaire ever change his bad-boy ways? Discover the answer in Miranda Lee's *The Guardian's Forbidden Mistress!* Susan Stephens brings you *Bought: One Island, One Bride,* where a Greek tycoon seduces a feisty beauty, then buys her body and soul. In *The Sicilian's Virgin Bride* by Sarah Morgan, Rocco Castellani tracks down his estranged wife—and will finally claim his virgin bride! In *Expecting His Love-Child,* Carol Marinelli tells the story of Millie, who is hiding a secret—she's pregnant with Levander's baby! In *The Billionaire's Marriage Mission* by Helen Brooks, it looks like wealthy Travis Black won't get what he wants for once—or will he? Finally, new author Christina Hollis brings you an innocent virgin who must give herself to an Italian tycoon for one night of unsurpassable passion, in her brilliant debut novel *One Night in his Bed.* Happy reading!

Dinner ^{at}8

Don't be late!

He's suave and sophisticated.

He's undeniably charming.

And, above all, he treats her like a lady....

But beneath the tux, there's a primal, passionate lover who's determined to make her his!

Wined, dined and swept away by a
British billionaire!

Helen Brooks

THE BILLIONAIRE'S MARRIAGE MISSION

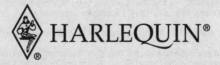

HARLEQUIN®

TORONTO • NEW YORK • LONDON
AMSTERDAM • PARIS • SYDNEY • HAMBURG
STOCKHOLM • ATHENS • TOKYO • MILAN • MADRID
PRAGUE • WARSAW • BUDAPEST • AUCKLAND

ISBN-13: 978-0-373-23469-1
ISBN-10:   0-373-23469-4

THE BILLIONAIRE'S MARRIAGE MISSION

First North American Publication 2008.

Copyright © 2006 by Helen Brooks.

All about the author...
Helen Brooks

HELEN BROOKS was born and educated in Northampton, England. She met her husband at the age of sixteen and, thirty-five years later, the magic is still there. They have three lovely children and a menagerie of animals in the house! The children, friends and pets all keep the house buzzing and the food cupboards empty, but Helen wouldn't have it any other way.

Helen began writing in 1990 as she approached that milestone of a birthday—forty! She realized her two teenage ambitions (writing a novel and learning to drive) had been lost amid babies and family life, so she set about resurrecting them. Her first novel was accepted after one rewrite, and she passed her driving test (the former was a joy and the latter an unmitigated nightmare).

Helen is a committed Christian and fervent animal lover. She finds that time is always at a premium, but somehow fits in walks in the countryside with her husband and dogs, meals out followed by the cinema or theater, reading, swimming and visiting with friends. She also enjoys sitting in her wonderfully therapeutic, rambling old garden in the sun with a glass of red wine (under the guise of resting while thinking, of course!).

Since becoming a full-time writer, Helen has found her occupation to be one of pure joy. She loves exploring what makes people tick, and finds the old adage that truth is stranger than fiction to be absolutely true. She would love to hear from any readers, care of Harlequin Presents.

CHAPTER ONE

As THE DOOR CLICKED gently shut behind her the quiet sound registered with all the force of a thunderclap on Beth Marton's ears. For a second she froze, unbelieving; then she turned, gingerly pushing against the unyielding wood. Of course it didn't budge—but then it wouldn't with the latch having sprung shut.

'Oh, no, no.' Beth pushed again, harder this time, even as she told herself it was pointless. She was locked out. If she had been standing outside her flat in London that wouldn't have mattered. There were at least a couple of neighbours always around that she could have called on in the block in which the flat was situated, and one of them could have telephoned her sister who had a spare key for emergencies. But this was not London...

She glanced somewhat wildly about her, vitally aware she was clad in nothing but bubblegum-pink silk pyjamas with spaghetti shoulder straps.

The dark windy night was not encouraging. And rain was forecast.

When a cold nose nudged one hand she glanced down at the big dog who was surveying her with impatient eyes. 'I know, I know,' she muttered. 'We're out here and your dinner's in there, but it was you who insisted you needed the loo a minute ago.'

And it was her who had followed Harvey outside with the torch so she could make sure he didn't disappear into the blackness. Which was doubly daft in hindsight, considering he knew it was dinner time—Harvey's favourite moment of the day—and also that there was nowhere he could really go. The garden surrounding the little cottage she was renting was all neatly fenced.

A gust of wind brought the smell of smoke on the air, reminding Beth she had lit the fire in the sitting room a few minutes before. And the guard wasn't in front of it but standing to one side of the slate hearth.

Panicking now, she scurried round the outside of the cottage to see if any of the windows just might be on the latch, although she doubted it. When she had arrived at the place half an hour ago, travel weary after a journey she wouldn't have wished on her worst enemy but hugely relieved to have found the isolated building in the dark, everything had appeared shuttered and closed. After retrieving the front door key which had been hidden under a plant pot as the agent had told her, she had lugged all her stuff inside, only stopping to bung perishable food into the little fridge before she had stripped off for a wonderfully welcome shower.

Once the stickiness of the tortuous journey—which had consisted of traffic jam after traffic jam—had been removed she hadn't been able to face the thought of dressing again, and so had pulled on her pyjamas before opening a bottle of wine and lighting the fire. Harvey's enormous basket established in a handy corner, and a tin of his favourite food open in the tiny cottage kitchen, she'd been about to feed him when he'd made it plain he needed to be let outside for a moment.

'Ow!' As she slipped on something squelchy and ended up on her bottom in something which smelt utterly disgusting, her eyeballs rattled with the jolt to her system. The urge to cry was suddenly and very childishly paramount, but instead she recovered the torch which had fallen out of her hand and struggled to her feet. Harvey seemed to have quite forgotten about his dinner and was entering into this new game with gusto, jumping about her and barking delightedly. He'd found the long journey from London to Shropshire boring but this was altogether more like it.

Thankfully the torch still worked, but Beth didn't need its light to tell her a fox or badger obviously skulked about the cottage garden at night. The smell on her pyjamas and fluffy mules did the job more than adequately.

Walking round the building to the front door again, she stood for a moment, shivering in the cold May night. The day itself had been quite warm, too warm in view of the hours spent stuck unmoving in traffic, but the night air had a bite to it which said summer wasn't quite round the corner yet.

She would have to smash a window and climb in somehow; there was nothing else for it. Beth gazed at the beautiful old leaded lights in the sitting room windows. All the glass was the same, and when she had drawn up earlier and admired the mullioned effect she had thought then they must be quite valuable. The cottage was tiny and chocolate boxy, complete with thatched roof, wooden beams throughout and all the charm one would expect considering it was a couple of centuries old. But charm didn't help her right at this minute.

Harvey's stomach was rumbling and the game had lost its appeal. He began to whine and when an enormous long-haired German shepherd dog whined it wasn't the same as a poodle. Beth couldn't hear herself think. 'All right, all right.'

She shushed him with a click of her fingers. She was going to do a considerable amount of damage if she smashed one of these lovely old windows but she couldn't think of any other course of action. As far as she could recall, she hadn't passed another dwelling place for some miles once she had turned into the long lane which had eventually led to the cottage. Besides which, she was hardly dressed to go tramping round the Shropshire countryside.

She shone the torch on the window as she pressed the glass. Each window was stone mullioned and the leaded lights appeared to be supported by steel bars behind them. She wasn't even sure she could climb in if she did manage to break the glass. Of course she could smash one of her car windows but she'd freeze to death in there tonight, and in the morning she'd still have the same problem, her car keys and everything else being in the cottage.

'Oh, Harvey.' The urge to cry was back. This, on top of everything else that had happened lately was too much. Why, when she was trying to pick herself up and sort herself out, was she hampered at every turn? It just wasn't *fair.* She sniffed miserably and Harvey, now sensing all was not well, pressed protectively against her legs. She plumped down on the doorstep and put her arms round the shaggy neck, tears running down her cheeks. And it was like that, huddled into the warm animal fur, that she first noticed moving lights on the hillside.

Someone was driving down the lane leading to the cottage!

Jumping up, she dashed past her car and the small area of lawn which made up the front garden and opened the big swing gate, holding Harvey's leather collar as she waited for whoever it was to reach them. She shone the torch anxiously into the road, hoping the vehicle owner wouldn't just drive straight past. It wasn't as if she looked as though she might be a dangerous mugger or something, she reasoned frantically, not in her pyjamas. But for that same reason she wanted any potential rescuer to see Harvey and know she had the sort of guard dog it wasn't wise to ignore. You heard such horrible things these days about women being attacked when they asked strangers for help.

It seemed an eternity before the car reached them but it could only have been a minute or two. Then brilliant headlights lit up the darkness, swallowing the meagre light from the torch. A large estate car swept by before Beth could blink. For an awful moment she thought the driver hadn't noticed them standing on the grass verge, but then she heard the screech of brakes after the car had disappeared from view round a bend in the road.

A few seconds later it reversed and came to a stop at the side of them.

The window wound down and a deep male voice, in tones of mingled amazement and amusement, drawled, 'What the dickens are you doing out here dressed like that?'

Enjoying myself? For a moment she almost let her tongue rule her brain before logic told her she had to get this guy on her side, whoever he was. Biting back the caustic retort which had sprung to her lips, she said evenly, 'I appear to have locked myself out when I was seeing to my dog. I don't suppose you've got anything in the car I could force the door with?' She swung the torch in the direction of his face as she spoke and saw him flinch as the bright light hit his eyes. 'Sorry.' She lowered it immediately but the brief glimpse had been enough to tell her the man was dark-haired and youngish; beyond that she hadn't been able to see.

'You're asking me to do a bit of breaking and entering?'

Amusement was definitely paramount now and Beth had to take a deep breath before she could say sweetly, 'I suppose so, yes. Can you help?' She was shivering from head to foot and in a minute her teeth would being to chatter, and this clown found the situation funny. The unfeeling so-and-so.

'You're cold.'

She hoped it was her shaking he had noticed and not the way her nipples were standing out like chapel hat pegs against the thin silk of her pyjama top. Not that she could do anything about it; she couldn't even cross her arms over her chest with one hand holding Harvey's collar and the other clutching the torch. 'A bit,' she said steadily. 'Which is why I'd like to get back in as soon as possible.'

The engine was turned off and the driver's door opened, a big figure uncurling itself from the dark depths of the vehicle. The next moment she was being handed a bulky jacket which must have been on the passenger seat beside him. 'Here, put this on,' he said easily, glancing down at Harvey who had begun a low rumbling growl in the back of his throat.

Beth didn't try to stop the dog; in fact she made a mental note to give him an extra handful of his favourite biscuits once they were inside. The man was tall—very tall—and intimidatingly broad-shouldered and muscular from what she could ascertain in the dim light. She didn't like to shine the torch up into his face again to get a good look at him but she was feeling distinctly nervous, being so scantily clad.

The next moment the stranger crouched down so that his head was in line with Harvey's powerful jaws, his voice relaxed and soothing as he said, 'Steady, boy. No one's going to harm your mistress,' and offered a hand for the dog to sniff.

There was a brief pause and then the rumbling stopped and a large pink tongue licked the man's hand as Harvey's tail wagged a greeting. Beth wondered if Harvey would look quite so pleased with himself if he knew he'd just blown the extra biscuits.

'Nice dog.' The man stood up and stretched out a hand, saying, 'Give me the torch while you put the coat on.'

Beth didn't see any point in arguing. If he was going to hit her over the head with something and have his wicked way with her, it might as well be the torch as anything else. Clearly Harvey was going to be no help whatsoever.

The man pushed past her and walked to the cottage door as she slipped the jacket on. It drowned her, but right at this moment that was very welcome. She followed him, Harvey trotting at her side, and watched as he first tried the door and then walked round the building checking each window as she'd done. Of course *he* didn't end up sitting in fox or badger dung.

When he re-emerged from the back of the cottage Beth said a little testily, 'I'd already tried all the windows.'

He didn't comment on this. What he did say was, 'What's that terrible smell? Raw sewage?'

'I slipped over at the back of the house. I think an animal had been there.'

'And how.' He didn't bother to try to hide his amusement.

She wasn't about to stand in the wind and cold discussing how she smelt. And he hadn't exactly been a gentleman to mention it in the first place. 'So, can you get me in?' she asked shortly. 'It's freezing out here.'

'Probably, but I don't intend to. There's no point in forcing the door or a window and causing a considerable amount of damage when you can contact the agent in the morning and ask them to call by. This place is rented by Turner & Turner, isn't it? The local estate agent?'

'Yes, but—'

'So I suggest you come back to my place and get a good night's sleep and we'll sort it in the morning. You haven't got anything on the stove in there, have you? Nothing's going to cause a problem?'

Was he mad? She would no more think of going back to 'his place' than flying to the moon. Stiffly now, Beth said, 'I lit a fire. I can't leave it.'

'You already have,' he pointed out silkily.

'The guard wasn't in front of it.'

'There's hardly any smoke coming out of the

chimney so it's probably dying out already. It'll be all right.'

So now he was an expert on fires? 'I can't possibly just walk away; you must see that?'

'Of course you can.' The comment about the estate agent had told her he must be a local, and this was confirmed now when he added, 'I know John Turner; I'll call him myself in the morning and explain the situation. You'll be back in by ten o'clock. He'd prefer that than breaking and entering, I'm sure.'

She didn't want to be back in by ten o'clock, she wanted to be back in *now*. 'If you know him, can't you phone now?'

She could see the silhouette of his head shaking as he said, 'No can do. Friday night is John's snooker night with the lads. Nothing gets in the way of that.'

This was absolutely ridiculous. 'I couldn't possibly go home with you, Mr…?'

'Black. Travis Black. Why couldn't you come home with me, Miss…?'

'My name's Beth Marton and I'm not in the habit of accepting overnight accommodation with complete strangers,' she said tightly, refusing to acknowledge Harvey, who had set himself down at the side of Travis Black for all the world as though he was his dog instead of hers. The traitor.

'We're not strangers, we've introduced ourselves.' It was lazy and the amusement was back tenfold. 'And rest assured I'm not so desperate for female company that I've seized on your unfortunate predicament with rape and pillage in mind. It's a genuine offer; you'll sleep alone, especially in view of that…unusual scent you're wearing.'

Swine. Dignity was hellishly difficult in view of the pink silk pyjamas and the smell, but Beth made a stab at it as she said crisply, 'Thank you for the offer but I couldn't, Mr Black. There's Harvey, for one thing.'

'I wasn't proposing you tie him up and leave him here. Of course he comes too.' He turned at this point, beginning to walk back to his car. 'Still, it's up to you.'

'Where are you going?' Beth knew her voice was too shrill but she couldn't help it. He wasn't going to just leave her here, was he? No one would be so hard-hearted…would they?

'Home.' He didn't bother to turn round. 'It's late and it's been a long day. I'm hungry, tired and it's beginning to rain. You can come with me or stay here—it's up to you.'

She didn't move until he had actually seated himself in the car; she couldn't quite believe he was just going to drive off. When he started the engine she admitted defeat, especially with the few spots of rain turning into a steady downpour.

She hurried across the garden to the gate, Harvey bounding at her heels, and tapped on the driver's window. It lowered. This time she kept the light just clear of his eyes but allowed the torch to give her a clear view of his face. It was an interesting face. Not handsome exactly—it was too rugged for that and the bright light showed up a scar on one chiselled cheekbone, but it had something which would make any red-blooded woman take a second glance. His hair was ebony-black but she couldn't determine the colour of his eyes with the brightness of the light distorting everything.

'I can't stay out here all night,' she muttered. 'There might not be anyone else pass by.'

'Sure fire bet,' he agreed pleasantly. 'My house is the only other building along here and the lane finishes at my front garden.'

And he had just been going to drive off knowing that? 'Where do I put Harvey?' she asked stiffly.

In reply he got out of the car and opened the back of the estate. Harvey jumped in and settled on the big blanket there as though he had been doing it all his life. Beth glared at the animal as Travis pulled the door down. He then walked round the vehicle and opened the passenger door for her without saying a word, but she just *knew* he was smiling inside.

She slid in. 'Thank you.' It was said through gritted teeth.

'My pleasure.' He closed the door very gently.

Once he had joined her in the car she became even more aware of the height and breadth of him and felt all the more vulnerable because of it. She also became rather more aware of the truly disgusting smell emanating from her clothes. 'I hope I don't spoil the seat,' she said in a small voice as the car began to move. She had noticed the car was a top of the range Mercedes Estate. She bet it was the first time the beautiful interior had been subjected to such abuse.

'It's leather; it'll sponge down if necessary. Once we get to my place you can have a shower and I'll sort out something clean for you to put on. It won't be pink, though,' he added, deadpan.

'Not your colour?' Beth asked in the same tone.

'Clashes with my eyes.' He grinned without looking at her.

'Right.' He was trying to put her at her ease. *And,* she reminded herself, he *was* providing a roof over her head for the night and if he hadn't come along she would have been in a real fix. 'This is very kind of you,' she said belatedly.

'That's me all over. Orphans, strays, lost sheep…'

'Yeah, right.' He was joking but the way she was feeling it was a little too near the mark. Beth forced all emotion out of her voice as she said, 'If yours is the only place on this road I was lucky you came along.'

'Especially as I don't live here all the time. I mostly work and live in Bristol.'

'Oh, yes?' She glanced at the hard profile. 'What do you do?' He wasn't the type of man you could easily pin a label on.

'Industrial design.'

That covered a thousand and one possible avenues, but as his voice had been dismissive Beth didn't like to ask what he specialised in. Instead she said, 'So your home here is a sort of weekend place?'

'More of a bolt-hole,' he said shortly. 'And you? Do you work?'

She nodded. 'Although I'm taking a break for a while. I'm an architect.'

She waited for the surprise which normally— and, as far as Beth was concerned, unflatter- ingly—followed this statement when she was talking to a man socially. As far as the male race seemed to think, the fact that she was slender and finely boned with honey-blonde hair and big blue eyes precluded her from having a profession which involved visiting construction sites and dealing with builders, among other things. The least of the offenders usually attempted to hide their amazement and say something like, 'Really? How interesting,' as they eyed her up and down blankly. The worst guffawed and said they didn't believe it.

Travis merely nodded. 'Work for a practice or local authority, or freelance?'

'A practice. They're holding my job for six months.'

She'd anticipated more questions but when none were forthcoming settled more easily into her seat, having become aware she was holding herself as taut as piano wire. The trees either side of the narrow lane formed a canopy overhead and the night was pitch black, the car's powerful headlights cutting through the darkness but somehow emphasising the loneliness of her surroundings. Her stomach kept flipping over like a pancake on Shrove Tuesday.

And then suddenly there were massive gates in front of them which Travis opened by remote control within the car. They drove through on to a pebbled drive and almost immediately the vista opened up and Beth saw a large house a hundred yards or so in the distance.

She didn't know what she had been expecting—probably a cottage similar to the one she was renting or something a little bigger—but it wasn't this mansion of a place in what was virtually a small park. She glanced at Travis—a quick look—but his eyes were on the windscreen. As bolt-holes went, this certainly wasn't the norm. Mind you, she was beginning to think Travis wasn't exactly the norm either, she thought ruefully.

Well-tended landscaped grounds stretched either side of the winding drive, and by the time they drew up in the horseshoe-shaped pebbled area in front of the house Beth had to admit privately to being somewhat overawed. Even if she had been dressed to the nines and perfectly coiffured she'd have felt a bit intimidated, she told herself silently. As it was…

Her thoughts made it all the more incongruous when Travis exited the car and walked round the bonnet to help her out of the vehicle as though they were on a date or something. She tried to be as graceful and dignified as present circumstances allowed—which wasn't saying much.

Outside lights situated at the front of the house had clicked on automatically as they'd arrived, but, flustered as she was, Beth had been concentrating on the absurdity of her situation rather than anything else. Now, as she slid out of the Mercedes with his warm hand supporting her, she looked at him—*really* looked at him—for the first time. A little bolt of electricity caused her breath to catch in her throat. Grey, she thought inconsequentially. His eyes are grey.

'What's the name of your dog?'

'What?' The cool voice had registered but her scrambled brain hadn't been able to compute.

'Your dog?' he repeated patiently.

She became aware of the barking. Harvey was taking exception to being stuck in the vehicle when they were outside. 'Oh, Harvey. His name's Harvey.'

'I suggest you get ready to reassure him. He'll be meeting my dogs in a moment and I'd prefer him to be friendly.'

The slight hiccup in her thought processes caused by the piercing quality of the deep grey eyes fringed by spiky black lashes evaporated. 'Harvey is *always* friendly,' she said tightly before she realised it didn't exactly reaffirm his guard dog persona.

'Good. Sheba and Sky aren't.'

The next moment he had opened the back of the estate car and Harvey had jumped down and, before she could ask him what he'd meant, he was turning the key in the lock of the front door. Immediately two grizzly bears—or that was what they looked like to Beth—bounded on to the drive.

There was a tense moment or two, on Beth's side, while the two dogs circled Harvey, but his wagging tail and lolling grin didn't falter. Within seconds the three dogs were inspecting each other's rear ends and introducing themselves. Beth sighed with relief. 'They're lovely,' she said unconvincingly, keeping her eye on the dogs in case they suddenly decided to go cannibal and give Harvey a hard time. 'What are they?'

'Apart from being female, I haven't a clue,' Travis said easily, clicking his fingers, at which signal both dogs shot to his side and sat down. 'They were dumped by the side of a road in a cardboard box at five or six weeks old. A friend of mine saw the incident and something made him go back and look inside the box. The vet reckons there's a number of breeds in there, but who's counting?'

Whatever their pedigree, Harvey seemed to find the two dogs attractive. Beth noticed he'd gone into macho man mode as he sauntered up to Travis and leered at the two females.

As they entered the house Beth's first impression was one of space and mellow wood. The large hall was oak floored, as was the wide curving staircase which led to a galleried first floor. The walls were light with several modern paintings providing vivid splashes of colour, and just a small oak table, either side of which stood two upholstered hardbacked chairs, broke the clean lines.

'I'm sure you'd like to shower and change

while I feed the dogs. Has Harvey been fed yet?' Travis was walking to the staircase as he spoke and his dogs stopped at the foot of it. Presumably they weren't allowed upstairs.

'No, he hasn't. I was just about to give him his food when we got locked out.' Beth followed Travis up the stairs after telling Harvey to stay. He made no objection, plonking himself firmly in the middle of the two females, where he appeared quite content. So much for the guard dog routine.

The oak floor continued along the galleried landing and, after leaning over to make sure Harvey was still behaving himself, Beth joined Travis where he was standing by an open bedroom door. 'You'll find some T-shirts and jogging bottoms in the wardrobe and a guest robe behind the bathroom door,' he said easily. 'Make yourself at home. There's plenty of hot water. When you're ready, come downstairs and find me in the kitchen. Do you like spaghetti Bolognese?'

'What? Oh, yes. Yes, thank you.' Terribly flustered, Beth stepped into the ankle-deep cream carpet of what was obviously a guest room and Travis shut the door behind her, leaving her alone. She gazed around her. The coffee and cream room had definitely been decorated and furnished by someone with minimalist taste, but it was beautiful. She suspected the whole house would be beautiful.

Gingerly, as though she was going to leave a trail of dirt and destruction, she made her way over to the open door of the en suite bathroom, which reflected the colours of the bedroom, and peered into the huge mirror stretching over a pair of basins.

She groaned out loud at the reflection staring back at her. Not only were her pyjamas and slippers the worse for wear, but a large smear of mud—at least she hoped it was merely mud and not what she'd slipped in—had deposited itself on the side of her face. Her hair had dried in a tangled riot in the wind and her make-up free face was shiny where it wasn't filthy. She looked like something the cat wouldn't deign to drag in. Not even if it was desperate.

Ten minutes later she felt more like herself. She had found face and body lotion along with shampoo and conditioner in the bathroom cabinet, and once she was clean, moisturised and sweet-smelling everything didn't seem so bad. After blow-drying her hair into its normal silky shoulder-length bob, she found some women's T-shirts and jogging bottoms neatly folded in a drawer in the otherwise empty wardrobe. Fleetingly she wondered who they belonged to. His girlfriend, maybe? she thought as she put her own things in water.

Right, time to face him again. She padded

downstairs in bare feet, aware that her stomach was jumping with trepidation, which was daft, really daft, but she didn't seem able to help it.

Once in the hall, she stared about her. Travis had said she should join him in the kitchen but there were several doors leading off the expanse in front of her. Assuming the kitchen was probably at the back of the house, she made her way down the hall towards the furthest door and knocked nervously before she opened it. 'Hello, it's me,' she said unnecessarily.

'Hi.' Travis was stirring something on the stove, the three dogs lying at his feet, apparently replete and content. Harvey wagged his tail at the sight of her but didn't bother to get up. 'Grab a seat,' Travis continued, 'and pour yourself a glass of wine.'

She was conscious of one piercingly thorough glance before he turned back to the stove. That, and the sight of the big powerful body clothed in a black cotton shirt, open at the neck, and black denim jeans was enough to make her all fingers and thumbs as she sat down at the big farmhouse-style kitchen table and reached for the open bottle of wine.

Large though the table was, it was swallowed by the roomy capaciousness of the kitchen. The stone-flagged floor, honey-coloured wooden cupboards and granite work surfaces looked like a blending of old with new but it was very pleasing to the eye.

The wine was very pleasing to the tastebuds. Deep red and with aromas of blackcurrant and cherry, Beth found it steadied her nerves nicely.

After several sips she was sufficiently calm to say evenly, 'Is there anything I can do to help?'

'Not a thing. It's ready.' Within a moment he had whisked two plates of spaghetti Bolognese over to the table along with a dish of lightly roasted vegetables. Beth's mouth watered. As Travis sat down he said matter-of-factly, 'You clean up nicely. More than nicely.'

'Thank you.' She knew she had turned an unflattering shade of red and it was annoying. It wasn't as though she was a stranger to compliments from the male of the species; it was just that this particular male was altogether…disturbing. Which was the last thing in the world she needed right now. 'And thanks for feeding us,' she added, indicating Harvey with a wave of her hand. 'I really didn't intend to put you to so much trouble when I waved you down earlier,' she finished primly.

The grey eyes surveyed her expressionlessly. In the bright light of the kitchen his face was rugged and attractive, full of very sharply defined planes and angles which the scar down one cheek heightened. His nose was straight, his thick brows and eyelashes the same coal black as his hair, and his mouth was sexy. This last thought was unwelcome but it was true. Travis Black exuded a cynical kind of sexiness that was over-whelmingly magnetic and Beth felt her toes curl with the force of it.

'We're neighbours,' he said lazily after a tense moment or two had crept by. 'Albeit temporarily. It was the least I could do. I'd hope someone would behave the same if my sister found herself stranded.'

He had a sister? Ridiculous, because probably mad axemen and all manner of ne'er-do-wells had sisters, but it was reassuring somehow. Beth hid behind a neutral social smile which could have meant anything as she studied him. 'How old is your sister?' she asked.

'Sandra? She had her thirtieth a few weeks ago. She's probably still celebrating, knowing Sandra. She's a party animal, to put it mildly.'

'You don't approve?' There had been something in his voice which had suggested this, although nothing she could put her finger on. But she could be wrong; he was as complete stranger after all.

He shrugged muscled shoulders, expertly forking a mouthful of spaghetti into his mouth and swallowing before he said lazily, 'She's a grown woman with a life of her own.'

It wasn't really an answer. Beth tried the Bolo-gnese. It was absolutely delicious. As cooking was one of her least favourite things, she'd always had enormous respect for someone who could take ordinary ingredients and turn them into something special. Her food varied between being overdone, underdone or just plain inedible.

'This is lovely,' she said a little grudgingly. Travis was clearly one of those men who would be good at anything he set his mind to. Like Keith. The thought brought her up sharp and she slammed shut that particular little door in her head and hung the 'do not enter' sign back in place.

'Thank you.'

There was a slightly quizzical note in his voice. Too late Beth realised her words probably didn't add up with the expression on her face. She smoothed out the frown and forced a smile. 'I can't cook for toffee,' she said lightly, 'and I'm always madly jealous of anyone who can.'

He nodded but said nothing. Beth got the distinct impression he hadn't believed her. She opened her mouth to say more and then shut it again, conscious that the old maxim of least said, soonest mended might ring true here. Anyway, she had never been a good liar. *Un*like Keith.

Reaching for her wine, she drained the glass, her knuckles tight round the stem. Relax, *relax,* she told herself silently.

Travis refilled it silently before leaning back in his chair and saying, 'Is it me or are you always this jumpy when you spend the night in a strange man's house?'

She smiled, more naturally this time. 'Are you strange?' she asked, falling in with his mood.

'It has been said in the past.' He grinned and the sexiness went up a few notches.

Beth told herself she had not noticed. 'Then I'll just have to watch my step.' She smiled again and then applied herself to the food. The sooner she finished the meal and could disappear upstairs to her room, the better. She didn't want to do friendly or flirty or anything else.

She ate quickly, keeping her eyes on her plate. It was great of him to step into the breach and offer her a bed for the night, she told herself silently, but she'd have been more than content to pay for the damage had he forced the cottage door or a window. And she would have much preferred that. Ungrateful, maybe, but that was how she felt.

'So are you renting the cottage for a full six months?'

They'd finished the food in silence and now, as Travis put down his fork and picked up his wine-glass, Beth nerved herself to meet the cool grey gaze. She nodded. 'That was the minimum period possible,' she said shortly.

'It's a very lonely location.'

'That's what I liked about it.' He was looking

at her in an uncomfortably speculative way and after a tense moment or two she added, 'I haven't been well recently. I wanted a complete change for a while.'

'You can't get more complete than Herb Cottage.'

Beth made no reply to this, finishing her wine and standing up quickly. 'If you don't mind, I'll turn in now,' she said awkwardly. 'It was an awful journey earlier and I'm tired.' She sounded boorish even to her own ears.

'I can't tempt you to some pudding?' Travis said mildly. 'There's hazelnut pie or apple crumble.'

She shook her head. 'No, thanks.' She glanced at Harvey, who hadn't moved so much as a paw. 'Where do you want him to sleep?'

'Oh, he'll bed down with the girls,' Travis said easily. 'He seems to have settled in just fine.'

Too fine in her opinion. Considering Harvey had been protective to the point where it could have been a problem over the last few months, he now seemed to have abandoned her. Feeling ridiculously put out, Beth said tensely, 'Well, thanks again. We'll be out of your hair as soon as possible in the morning.'

'There's no rush.'

Oh, yes there was. He had stood up when she'd risen and he looked very big and very male. And attractive. Definitely attractive. Appalled by the direction her thoughts were taking, Beth told herself she was overtired. 'Goodnight,' she mumbled hastily and fled the kitchen before he even had a chance to reply.

CHAPTER TWO

THE BED WAS supremely comfortable, it was quiet and peaceful and she was as warm as toast. Beth turned over for the umpteenth time and asked herself why she couldn't sleep. She was exhausted, there was no doubt about that, but her mind was buzzing. She groaned softly and buried her face in the pillow, getting more annoyed with herself with each passing moment.

She didn't want to think about Keith and normally she could keep him very firmly at bay these days, so why was she raking up old wounds tonight? She'd thought she was past all that.

It was him—Travis Black. He reminded her of Keith. If she was being honest, however, she couldn't think why. Certainly the two men were not alike physically. Keith was blond and blue-eyed with a warm boyish smile and a totally unthreatening masculinity which had nevertheless been very engaging. She had fallen head over heels in love with him the first moment they had met when he'd walked into the office. And he'd said he'd felt the same—had said he adored her, worshipped her.

Stupid. Beth sat up abruptly and ran her fingers through her rumpled hair. Really, really stupid. She should have known that a successful, handsome entrepreneur like Keith Wright would have more strings to his bow than a company of concert violinists. But she had trusted him. She had loved him and she'd trusted him, it was as simple as that. Biggest mistake of her life.

Come on, stop this. You're over the worst, you don't do post mortems on Keith any more. The admonition was there in her mind but tonight she couldn't stem the memories flooding in.

They'd had a low-key wedding. Keith had wanted it that way and she had been so gloriously happy she'd have got married in sackcloth and ashes if he'd asked her to. As it was, she'd worn a powder-blue suit and large hat, and everyone had said she looked radiant.

Keith had whisked her off to the Bahamas for two weeks and they had returned to live in his modern apartment on the outskirts of London. The original plan had been to start looking for a house straight away, but as the weeks and months had slipped by it had never happened. Keith had said there was plenty of time and she had agreed with him. When they decided to start trying for a baby in the future, they would think about a house. Until then they were happy as they were.

And then one terrible night her sister and brother-in-law, Michael, had turned up at their apartment. White-faced and trembling from head to foot, Catherine had told her their beloved parents had been killed in a head-on collision. Two eighteen-year-old joyriders in a stolen car had veered across the motorway, causing a lorry to swerve to avoid them. In doing so, the lorry driver had lost control of his vehicle and her parents had ploughed into it. The lorry driver had cuts and bruises and the joyriders not a scratch. Neither had they any remorse. The case had attracted nationwide publicity, as much because one of the joyriders had a famous rock star brother as anything else.

A day or two after she and Keith and Catherine and Michael had been interviewed by the press on the steps of the courthouse at the finish of the trial, the joyriders having received the maximum sentence possible, she had returned home from work to find a young woman waiting outside the apartment.

The recent past, as she and Catherine had battled to come to terms with the sudden loss of their parents, had been bad enough, but nothing could have prepared her for what had followed. The young woman was Keith's long-term partner. They had two children and had been living together for seven years. On the nights he had been 'away' on business he had, in fact, been on the other side of London with Anna. And there were girlfriends too, Anna had told her in a bitter rage. There always had been. Anna had turned a blind eye to Keith's women because she loved him and he was the father of her little girls, but when she had seen him on the news with a *wife*... Only the day before he had left them all with hugs and kisses after spending the night in her arms. She'd had no idea he had actually *married* someone else.

Beth had stared at the distraught young woman as her world had come crashing down about her ears. She had believed Anna instantly. Later she'd questioned why and had come to the conclusion that as Anna had spoken a thousand and one little things had suddenly come into sharp focus, starting with their quiet no-fuss wedding twelve months before. And a couple of days before Christmas he had supposedly had to fly up to Scotland on business and had been unable to make it back to her before Boxing Day. Of course he had spent Christmas Eve and Christmas Day with

Anna and his children. Wheels within wheels and so cunning.

The more she and Anna had spoken, the more she had realised just how devious Keith had been. He had walked in on them some time later and if ever she'd needed confirmation that Anna was speaking the truth, the look of horror on Keith's face was it.

She had walked out that same night and had never gone back except to pick up a few personal belongings with Catherine when Keith had been at work. She had refused to see or speak to him and once he had realised she was deadly serious he had not contested the divorce. But then he couldn't have, not with her evidence.

Catherine and Michael had been wonderful, insisting she stay with them, but as Catherine was pregnant with their first child she had only stayed a short while. As soon as she was able she had found a small one-bedroom flat and bought it outright with her half of the inheritance from her parents' estate. It had taken every last penny but she had needed to know she had her own home. The day after she'd moved in Catherine and Michael had turned up on the doorstep with Harvey, who had been nothing more than a bundle of fluff with outsize paws and a pink tongue.

'A housewarming present,' Catherine had announced. 'And now I've left work I can look after him on the days when you're in the office. You need company at night. OK?'

She had protested she didn't want a dog and that it wouldn't be practical, but she knew Catherine was worried to death about her and convinced she'd sink into a bog of despair once she was alone and it had been that which had persuaded her to take Harvey. As it was, it had turned out that Catherine was absolutely right. She didn't know how she would have got through the last tortuous eighteen months without him. And there was something immensely reassuring in having Harvey with her at night and taking him to some of the more isolated sites she had to visit. He was so fiercely protective of her. He was also as good as gold with Catherine and the baby on the days she was confined to the office.

And so, with Harvey's help, she had battled on until a few weeks ago when the combined pressure of grief over the loss of her parents, Keith's betrayal and the breakdown of her marriage, plus the fact she'd been working too hard since the divorce had finally caught up with her. According to the doctor, she had suffered some kind of mini breakdown and needed a complete rest.

She had flatly refused to take the medication

he'd prescribed but had acknowledged an extended holiday would be no bad thing. Somewhere totally quiet and isolated, she'd decided. A step out of time. Somewhere she could learn to sleep properly again and regain her appetite, where she didn't have to see a soul if she didn't want to. She'd put her requirements with several estate agents and when Herb Cottage had come to her attention she had known she'd found her little piece of English heaven.

English heaven! Beth snorted out loud, swinging her feet out of bed and walking into the *en suite* bathroom, where she poured herself a glass of water. It hadn't seemed like heaven tonight, standing in the wind and cold. Once she was back in the cottage tomorrow she would go and get an extra key cut in the nearest town and hide it in the garden so there was never a repeat performance of this travesty. She still couldn't believe she'd been so stupid.

She drank the water and climbed back into bed, leaving the bedside lamp on. This was a beautiful room. She glanced about her before sliding back under the duvet and determinedly shutting her eyes. It was a beautiful house altogether. Did Travis Black often bring his girlfriends here for a romantic weekend? No doubt he had plenty of women to choose from; he was that kind of man. They'd be queueing up in their droves.

In the shadowed darkness her lip curled. She bet he knew all the right things to say, like Keith had. Men always knew what to say to get what they wanted but they weren't to be trusted. They said one thing and meant another. At least a certain type of man did, and very often ones who had an extra something that was hard to define but which was very real.

She turned over in bed, bringing the pillow over her head as though she could shut out her thoughts that way. And it was like that, virtually buried in the downy softness, that she finally went to sleep, but not before the first rays of morning were beginning to streak across a charcoal sky.

Beth was woken the next morning by a loud scratching at the bedroom door followed by a sharp knock. She sat bolt upright, her heart pounding and momentarily disorientated until in the next moment she remembered. She'd been locked out; this was Travis Black's house. Her heart pounded even harder.

When the knock came again she pulled herself together, making sure the duvet was up round her chin—in spite of having slept in the jogging bottoms and T-shirt—as she called, 'Come in.'

'Hi.' As the door opened she was conscious of Travis's voice but it was Harvey jumping on to the bed that took all her attention. The big dog plonked his massive paws on her shoulders and proceeded to lick her face anxiously in spite of her protests. When she finally managed to push him away it was to see Travis at the side of the bed with a tray. His voice amused, he said, 'Harvey's been whining and pacing the kitchen for the last hour. I think he thought you'd run off and left him.'

Great. After cheerfully waving her off to goodness knew where the night before, Harvey had finally remembered his obligations at a time when her hair looked like a bird's nest and her face hadn't woken up. Of course it wouldn't have mattered if it had just been Harvey finding her but he'd had to go and bring Travis Black too! Talk about adding insult to injury.

Beth nerved herself to glance at Travis. He was wearing jeans and an open-necked cream shirt. He was freshly shaved and the black hair was still damp from the shower. Narrow-waisted and lean-hipped with shoulders broad enough for even the most picky female, his aura of maleness was over-whelming. She felt at such a disadvantage that speech seemed to have deserted her. She swallowed hard, wishing she was a natural wit.

Travis didn't seem to have noticed. Or maybe he thought she was always this gormless. Beth tried to think of something to say and failed miserably.

'I wasn't sure if you took tea or coffee first thing.' Travis nodded to the contents of the tray. There was a mug of both along with sugar, milk and a small plate of plain biscuits. 'Breakfast will be ready in half an hour, OK?'

'Oh, please, don't go to any trouble. I'll just phone the agent guy if you give me his number and get out of your hair. I've imposed on you enough.' Aware she was babbling, Beth came to an abrupt halt. From not getting started, now she couldn't stop. He must be wondering what he'd taken on.

Deep grey eyes surveyed her unblinkingly. 'I've already talked to John and he's meeting us at the cottage at eleven. Hash browns or sauté potatoes with your cooked breakfast?'

'What?' He was close enough for her to scent his male warmth and the faintest tang of delicious aftershave. It was doing crazy things to her hormones. 'Oh, hash browns, please,' she managed weakly. Control. This was all about control.

He nodded, placing the tray on the bedside cabinet before walking to the door. Harvey trotted along with him. Clearly the big dog had decided that as she was alive and well he'd rather get back to his canine companions while the going was good.

Once the door had closed behind the pair of them, Beth leapt out of bed and inspected her reflection in the bathroom mirror. She groaned. The man was forever destined to see her looking as though she had been pulled through a hedge backwards.

Not that it mattered, she told herself firmly in the next moment. Of course it didn't. Travis Black was nothing to her and after today she would probably only catch a glimpse of his car, if anything, as it passed in the lane outside Herb Cottage. It was just that in spite of her life being a shambles she still had her self-respect and pride in her appearance.

She grimaced at the face in the mirror and turned away, walking back into the bedroom and drinking her coffee at the bedroom window. The room was situated at the back of the house and the view outside was tremendous. The grounds belonging to Travis were extensive and well cared for, smooth green lawns and mature trees and shrubs competing with large flowerbeds which were a riot of colour in the bright sunlight. But beyond the dry stone wall which bordered the property there was a rolling vista of trees, fields and hedges which stretched for miles, hills and valleys losing their separate identity as they stretched into infinity.

'Gorgeous.' Beth breathed out the word, her eyes focusing on a little flock of long-tailed tits flitting delicately in the branches of one of the beech trees close to the house. There was all the peace and tranquillity you could ever wish for. Which made it all the more surprising somehow that Travis lived here, albeit only part-time. He gave the impression of being a man who would always want to keep his finger on the pulse and be where the action was.

And then she frowned to herself. She didn't usually make assumptions about people and yet she couldn't seem to stop where Travis was concerned. Mentally shaking the unsettling feeling away, she finished the coffee and went into the bathroom for a shower. She'd feel better when she looked human again.

Twenty minutes later she made her way downstairs, her hair a shining curtain either side of her face and smelling of apple blossom from the shampoo she'd found in the bathroom cabinet. Without any perfume or even so much as a lip gloss in the way of make-up, it was the best she could do, she thought ruefully. In fact she felt remarkably bohemian with bare feet and a bare face, not to mention her lack of underclothes under the jogging bottoms and T-shirt. She always dressed very smartly for work, even when she was going on site—donning wellington boots and the big shapeless cagoule she kept in the car, she made sure the clothes beneath were immaculate.

Power dressing, Keith had used to call it. Not

exactly in a nasty way but with some amusement. She had countered this by insisting that in the male dominated world of her profession the image she projected was all important. Her blonde hair, blue eyes and feminine curves were enough to cause some men to doubt her brain power—she wasn't going to dress girly-girly to give them more ammunition. Not that they ever made the same mistake twice, she thought grimly. Not by the time she'd finished with them.

In a repeat of the night before, Travis was standing at the stove as she entered the kitchen, the three dogs spread out at his feet. Beth forced her voice into bright and breezy mode. 'That smells lovely.'

He smiled. Beth wondered why it was that when some men smiled they just smiled, and with others it was like *pow*. Travis's smile was a definite pow plus.

'I thought we'd eat in here again, if that's OK?' he said easily. 'I do actually have a dining room, believe it or not, but this is more…relaxed.'

Was that another way of saying this was in no way, shape or form anything remotely resembling a date and she mustn't get the wrong idea about his hospitality? Beth sat down at the kitchen table. If so, that suited her just fine. 'With a kitchen as nice as this one I should think you eat in here all the time,' she said carefully. 'I would.'

'Quite a bit,' he said, forking bacon into a dish.

There was already a coffee-pot, orange juice, toast and preserves on the table. Now Travis deftly placed dishes containing scrambled eggs, sausages, bacon, fried tomatoes, hash browns and various other items of food alongside them. Beth thought there was enough to feed an army. She gazed at it in alarm.

'Help yourself.' He joined her at the table and immediately her senses tingled at his nearness. Which was annoying, really annoying. Especially as he was totally laid-back.

'Thanks.' For the last few months she hadn't had anything of an appetite and had had to force herself to eat, often as not. It was with some surprise that she suddenly found she was quite hungry. She piled up her plate and began eating.

The food tasted as good as it looked. The sausages and bacon were crisp where they should be crisp but juicy where they needed to be. The rest of the breakfast was also perfect.

Beth had just popped the last morsel of egg in her mouth and leant back in her chair, feeling utterly replete, when she became aware that Travis was staring at her with unconcealed fascination. But not the 'I fancy you like mad' kind as his words informed her when he said, 'For such a tiny little thing you can certainly pack it away when you want to, can't you?'

She wasn't sure if it was a compliment or an insult. Warily she said, 'It must be the country air; I don't usually eat much, actually. Little and often suits me best.'

'It wasn't a criticism.'

His smoky voice held amusement and she felt herself flush. 'I didn't think it was.' She met the grey gaze head-on.

'No?' His brows rose mockingly.

'No.' It was very firm. Too firm?

'Good.' He clearly didn't believe her. 'I can't stand women who nibble on a lettuce leaf all day, as it happens,' he said lazily, standing and beginning to clear the empty dishes into the dishwasher. 'Incredibly irritating.'

I bet they're the sort you date, though, Beth thought sourly. Gorgeous model types who would look good in anything. He turned and caught the look on her face before she could wipe it away. He seemed to have a talent for catching her unawares.

Stopping what he was doing, he leant back against the worktop and folded his arms. 'You don't like me,' he said thoughtfully. 'Why is that, Beth?'

She could feel her ears burning. Mortified, she mumbled, 'I don't know you, so how could I dislike you? And you've been very kind, taking me and Harvey in, feeding us and everything.'

He made a cutting motion with his hand but his voice was still contemplative rather than concerned when he said, 'I thought last night you were nervous because of the position you were in and I could understand that. A stranger, the two of us alone here…' The grey eyes wandered over her hot face.

In spite of her acute discomfort, Beth registered that eyelashes the length and thickness of his were wasted on a man.

'But it's not that, is it? It's me. You don't like *me*.'

He didn't sound at all bothered. Pique added itself to embarrassment. 'As I said, I don't know you.'

He reached for a dish on the table in which three sausages remained. Giving one to each of the three dogs, he placed the empty container in the dishwasher before he said, 'You don't lie very well, Beth Marton.'

'I'm not a man, am I?' It was out before she even had time to think. Damn, damn, *damn*. She flushed hotly.

The piercing gaze homed in. There was an earsplitting moment of silence before he said, very quietly, 'I see.'

She wanted to run but she kept her voice low as she stared at him defiantly. 'What does that mean?'

He took up the challenge immediately. 'It's the answer to why a young woman with your looks and brains is burying herself in the back of beyond for a while,' he said calmly.

Arrogant, self-opinionated, supercilious swine. 'You know nothing about me, Mr Black, so don't pretend you do.'

'The name's Travis,' he said mildly, glancing at his watch before adding, 'And we'd better be making tracks if we're going to meet John. I've dug out a pair of old flip-flops my sister left here some time ago, by the way. I presume you don't want to wade through mud if you don't have to?'

It was through gritted teeth that she said, 'Thank you.'

'You're most welcome.' He bowed his head, his eyes on her.

He was enjoying this. She just knew he was enjoying the whole situation. Beth rose with what she hoped was a good deal of dignity. 'I'll go and fetch my things from upstairs.' She paused. Much as she hated to ask, she couldn't very well let her pyjamas and slippers drip all over his carpet. 'Do you have a carrier bag I can use?' she added tightly. 'I left my clothes in soak last night.'

'Very wise.' He reached into a cupboard and fetched out a bag. 'And the flip-flops are by the front door.'

She nodded and then sailed out of the room with her nose in the air. Once in her bedroom, she closed the door and leaned against it, shutting her eyes for a moment. All this because she had made the mistake of following Harvey outside to make sure he was all right. She must have been mad. If ever a dog could look after himself, Harvey could.

Levering herself upright, she marched into the bathroom and retrieved her sodden pyjamas and slippers from the basin. They still carried a faint whiff of something unmentionable.

'It doesn't matter,' she told herself out loud. 'Just keep calm and ignore anything he might say. In a little while you'll be back in the cottage and you need never see Travis Black again in the whole of your life.'

And that couldn't happen a moment too soon as far as she was concerned. He might have rescued her—in a fashion—and in a way she supposed he was something of a good Samaritan, albeit a slightly sarcastic and head-on challenging one, but he was right. She didn't like him. He was too self-assured, too high-handed, and that amusement with which he seemed to view her was downright insulting.

She was a capable and experienced professional woman who held down a good job and took care of herself just fine. Well, usually. Admittedly last night had been something of a hiccup but everyone had those now and again. He seemed to think she was an empty airhead.

She stuffed her wet things into the bag, frowning fiercely. And now she had to face this John Turner, who undoubtedly would also think she was a dizzy female who had lost the sense she was born with. Life was so *unfair* sometimes…

CHAPTER THREE

A ROSY-FACED LITTLE roly-poly figure of a man was waiting outside the cottage when they arrived a short time later. He raised a cheerful hand in greeting, beaming, as they exited the Mercedes, apparently not in the least put out at having his Saturday morning messed up.

'Hello, there!' His jovial voice matched his appearance. 'What a to-do, eh?' he said directly to Travis, adding, 'and you must be Miss Marton? Pleased to meet you, m'dear.'

'I'm sorry about this.' As Beth shook the little man's hand she was red with embarrassment. Not so much at having to call the estate agent out but more because she had noticed the somewhat speculative glance he had shot at Travis. John Turner had obviously put two and two together and made ten regarding her overnight stay.

'Not to worry. It's easy done, locking yourself out. My wife does it all the time. Now, let's get you

back inside, shall we?' He swung round and
opened the front door with the key in his hand,
adding over his shoulder, 'You coming to the
football this afternoon, Travis? Looks like it'll be
a good match.'

'Possibly.' As John Turner stood aside for her
to enter the cottage, Travis remained standing
where he was.

'Thank you for helping last night.' Flustered,
Beth snapped her fingers at Harvey, who had been
sniffing round the garden as she added, 'Would
either of you like a coffee before you go?'

'Not for me, thanks. Million and one things to do.'
The estate agent was already walking back to his car.

Beth turned to look at Travis, convinced he
would want to come in and mentally willing him
to say no. And then, when he did just that, she felt
a totally unreasonable dart of pique.

'If you need my services again, just don those
pink silk things and wave me down,' Travis added,
deadpan, before turning and beginning to walk
away.

Beth stared after him. He was going? Just like
that? But then, why wouldn't he? She had made
it pretty clear she couldn't wait to see the back of
him, after all. But still… 'These clothes,' she
called after him. 'When will you be around so I
can pop them back to you after I've washed them?'

He turned at the gate, surveying her through slits of brilliant grey light for a moment or two, his face expressionless. 'Don't worry about it,' he said lazily. 'Sandra has umpteen pairs of jogging bottoms and T-shirts; she won't miss those.'

They were his sister's clothes? The fact that this gave her satisfaction was a warning in itself. 'I couldn't possibly keep them,' she said primly. 'I must drop them by at some point.'

He shrugged. 'There's a mail box just outside the gates for any letters and parcels that get delivered when I'm up here. It's always unlocked. Drop them in there if you must.' His tone stated she was being unnecessarily pedantic.

'Right.' She nodded briskly, masking the umbrage she was feeling at his complete disinclination to any more contact. 'I'll do that.' Harvey was whining slightly at her side and she kept her hand on his collar. The dog obviously didn't want to see Travis leave and she wouldn't put it past Harvey to go galloping after him if she let go. 'Goodbye, then.'

'Goodbye, Beth,' Travis said softly. 'It was nice meeting you.'

The rest of the day was a definite anticlimax. It didn't take more than half an hour to settle in to her temporary new home and, after raking out the ashes of the fire and laying a new one ready to be lit that evening, Beth took Harvey for a long walk in the woods surrounding the property.

The May day was another warm one and after a couple of hours the path they were following dropped steeply beside a tiny stream that burrowed its way out of the hillside. Beth sat on the grassy bank as Harvey cavorted in the water, his splashing offending the birds in the trees surrounding them, who showed their displeasure by giving alarm calls and the odd bout of mad fluttering.

In spite of Harvey's antics it was very peaceful. Beth, her back resting against an ancient oak tree, allowed her mind to wander, and it was a full minute before she realised that all she was thinking about was Travis Black. Which was crazy—worse than crazy. She didn't know what had got into her.

She sat up straight, annoyed with herself. He had been kind, she had to give him that, but the whole episode was now a closed chapter, so why was she wasting one second thinking about a virtual stranger? And a much too attractive stranger at that. Travis was the sort of man who ought to have 'Danger to Women' stamped across his forehead in big red letters.

Harvey decided to come and shake himself at her side in the next moment, which effectively cut

Beth's musings short, but for the rest of the walk she made sure Travis was kept firmly on the perimeter of her thoughts. It was a battle, but she managed it.

A golden twilight was scenting the air when Beth finally pushed open the gate of Herb Cottage much later that day. She was exhausted, but pleasantly so. Harvey was making it clear he felt his paws had been walked off and that he was ready for his dinner as he plodded after her.

She saw the big bunch of flowers lying on the doorstep almost immediately, her pulse quickening as she walked up the garden path. The pale pink rosebuds, freesias and baby's breath were wrapped in cellophane and tied with a pink ribbon. The small card read, 'A little housewarming present'. It was signed simply 'Travis'.

She stared at the firm black scrawl, her heart thumping. He had bought her flowers. It was the last thing she'd expected after their somewhat terse parting. Why had he done that?

She opened the door, clicking the latch down once she was in the cottage so there couldn't be a repeat of last night's performance. Walking into the tiny kitchen, she lay the flowers on the draining board, continuing to stare at them until Harvey's whine reminded her he was waiting for his meal.

Once the dog was fed, she dug out a vase from

the bits and pieces in the cupboard under the sink and placed the flowers in water. They were gorgeous, absolutely gorgeous.

They didn't mean anything; he was probably just being kind. She nodded at the thought. Which was fine. People were allowed to be kind without any ulterior motives, after all. These flowers didn't mean he was interested in her. She frowned at the sweetly scented blooms as she carried the vase through to the sitting room. But his doing this was a…complication.

She plonked the vase down on the old-fashioned dresser and went to fix herself a quick meal of salad and cold meat. She ate her supper on a tray in the sitting room, staring at the flowers, Harvey sitting to attention at her feet as he eyed her last piece of home-cured ham hopefully.

The flowers didn't mean she would necessarily see anything of Travis Black again, she told herself later as she washed the dishes before getting ready for bed. From what he'd told her, he was a busy man and time was at a premium. And, as she didn't want to see him again, that suited her perfectly.

Nevertheless, in the short time before she drifted off to sleep, she couldn't help anticipating the next day and whether there would be a knock at the door. And she didn't like the way her pulse quickened at the possibility either.

* * *

There was no knock at the door, not on the following day or the subsequent ones. Travis had obviously returned to Bristol after his weekend at his bolt-hole. Beth told herself she was immensely relieved that a difficult episode had finished on a good note, and she was, in a way. She didn't want to see Travis again—she didn't want to get mixed up with any man again—so she couldn't quite understand why she found him popping into her mind at odd moments.

She washed and ironed the T-shirt and jogging bottoms and packaged them up with a note thanking him for his hospitality and the gift of the flowers, depositing the parcel in the post box he'd spoken of on Saturday morning. Once that was done she felt a little better about everything. She had kept the note polite and friendly but faintly dismissive, covertly indicating she didn't expect their paths to cross again.

As one peaceful May day after another passed, Beth found herself eating and sleeping better than she had in years. This was partly due to the peace and quiet, but also because the days were sunny and warm and she and Harvey could tramp the countryside to their hearts' content, returning home tired and happy as evening shadows stretched across the cottage garden.

Green valleys and wooded hillsides, little grey

farms and whitewashed cottages provided surroundings so different from the clamour and bustle of London that Beth felt she'd been transported to another world rather than a different part of England. She seemed to come across something enchantingly different almost every day. A buzzard soaring from a rocky crag, a brood of baby ducklings swimming in a little pool amidst the heather, ponies frolicking and chasing each other by the side of a dashing stream and the delicate pale rosettes of butterwort leaves on a green river bank.

It all worked a magic she had desperately needed. As her skin took on a golden glow from the sun and her blonde hair turned a shade lighter, so her mind was renewed. Suddenly the thought of tomorrow was exciting and pleasurable rather than something to be got through with gritted teeth and a determined smile. Here she didn't have to pretend to anyone. She shopped locally but, apart from politely passing the time of day with the shopkeepers, kept herself to herself. In London she had been the most gregarious of souls, here she was positively hermit-like. But it was wonderful, liberating. She felt reborn.

And so the month of May passed, June coming in on the crest of a heatwave as the weather turned even warmer.

It was on the second of the month, some three

weeks after she had moved to Shropshire, that Beth saw the Mercedes snaking its way past the cottage one Friday evening as she was throwing a ball for Harvey in the garden. She froze, her eyes following the vehicle as it disappeared from sight without stopping.

As far as she knew, Travis hadn't been around since that first night. She supposed he might have been, but she hadn't seen anything of him.

Harvey barked to remind her to continue with the game but now she did so mechanically, suddenly feeling all on edge. Which was ridiculous, plain daft in fact, but she couldn't help it.

Had he noticed her in the garden? She became aware that she was in a pair of her oldest jeans and a thin vest top, make-upless and with her hair bundled into a high ponytail to keep her neck cool. She looked a mess.

As the realisation hit her, Beth hurried back into the house but there brought herself up short. She was *not* going to change or brush her hair or anything else. What on earth was the matter with her? He wouldn't come to see her anyway.

Deliberately she made herself go into the kitchen, pouring herself a glass of wine and then walking through into the tiny back garden, which was only big enough to hold a profusion of flower-filled tubs and an old wooden bench. It was a sun-trap though, and she often spent the last daylight hours lazily watching fat honey-bees buzzing busily from flower to flower.

Harvey flung himself down at her feet and promptly started to snooze, twitching and whining in his sleep now and again as he dreamt. Beth envied his placid equanimity.

It could only have been twenty minutes later when the knock came at the front door. She couldn't pretend she hadn't heard it, not with Harvey waking up with a start and barking his head off. Setting her glass down, she forced herself to walk calmly into the house and through to the front door. Taking a long deep breath, she opened it. She had no doubt who it would be.

'Hi.' Unlike her, Travis looked unruffled and cool, his dark blue shirt open at the neck and his light cotton trousers crease-free. 'Neighbourly visit to see how you're doing,' he drawled easily. 'How are you? Everything OK?'

'Me? Oh, I'm great, thanks.' She knew she'd gone brick-red and it was utterly humiliating, especially in view of his aura of relaxed self-confidence. She'd just forgotten how big and attractive he was. 'Would…would you like to come in for a minute?' she asked reluctantly when he didn't say anything else.

'Thanks.' He followed her into the cottage,

Harvey bouncing about delightedly at the reunion. Immediately the cottage seemed to shrink. 'This is cosy,' he said, glancing around.

'I'm having a glass of wine in the garden. Care to join me?' Beth hoped she sounded less flustered than she felt.

'Sounds good.' He smiled slowly and her pulse accelerated.

She all but scampered through to the kitchen away from his disturbing presence, remembering belatedly that the bench was the only seat in the back garden and whereas it was fine for one it was a mite too cosy for two. He stood in the doorway as she found another glass and poured the wine, the piercing grey eyes on her hot face. Beth felt all fingers and thumbs.

'Thanks.' He took the glass and stood aside for her to go into the garden. Suddenly she seemed to have forgotten how to walk. Annoyed with herself, she led the way.

Once outside, Beth waved towards the bench. 'Please sit down,' she said as casually as she could, picking up her glass and perching somewhat precariously on the edge of one of the tubs of greenery opposite the bench. 'And thanks again for the flowers,' she added, 'but you shouldn't have.'

'Shouldn't I?' He sat with one arm stretched along the back of the bench, one leg crossed over the other knee. It was a very masculine pose. But then Travis was a very masculine man, she thought inanely. 'Why is that?'

'Why…' For a moment her brain scrambled. Then she said quickly, 'After all you'd done to help, it should have been me buying you something to say thank you.'

He smiled, shrugging his shoulders. 'I think not. All I did was provide a bed for the night.'

She hoped her nose wasn't shiny but ten to one it was. It also felt a little sunburnt and was probably glowing like a beacon. She tried to ignore the effect his smoky voice had on her nerve-endings as she said, 'Nevertheless I don't know what I'd have done if you hadn't happened by. It was a ridiculous position to be in. I'm not normally a fluttery type of female.'

Travis didn't reply to this. What he did say was, 'And you're feeling better now?'

'Better?' She stared at him warily. 'I don't understand.'

'You said you'd taken the cottage for a while because you had been ill,' he reminded her gently. 'I wondered if you were feeling it was doing you good.'

'Oh, I'm fine now,' she said firmly. 'Back to normal.'

'Overwork, was it?' The black eyebrows were enquiring.

She hadn't expected him to push the point and it took her aback so she didn't answer immediately. It was when she saw his eyes narrow that she forced herself to say, 'Partly, yes,' in as cool a voice as she could manage without being offensive. There was absolutely no way she was going to discuss her past with Travis Black. No way. With this in mind, she added, 'It was peace and quiet I wanted and this cottage provides it. No having to be up at the crack of dawn to fight my way through London traffic, no deadlines, no arguing with builders or trying to appease clients, no people. I don't have to see a soul here and that's the way I like it.' Big hint there. Take it.

The slight quirk to the firm mouth told her her covert message had been received and understood. He was a trespasser, an unwelcome intruder into her small world. Beth refused to feel guilty. She hadn't asked him to come here today. She *had* asked for his help that night three weeks ago but she'd had no option then, and she had thanked him for his assistance more than once. She decided not to follow this train of thought because it was making the refusal to feel guilty harder to maintain and she needed to be strong around this man.

'At least you've provided a spark of excitement

hereabouts,' Travis said drily. 'You're the talk of the village. Did you know that? Everyone's consumed by curiosity, apparently.'

Beth showed her alarm. 'Why is anyone interested in me?'

'A beautiful mystery woman who takes a cottage in the middle of nowhere and lives the life of a recluse. Why do you think?' he said softly. 'All the hallmarks of a good book.'

Beth stared at the dark craggy face. He was enjoying this, enjoying needling her, she thought, watching him as he swallowed the last of his wine. She was blowed if she was going to offer him another glass. She adopted the face and posture which always worked with difficult builders or clients and said crisply, 'I'm sorry people haven't got anything better to talk about. They must lead very boring lives round here.'

It was like water off a duck's back to Travis. He looked down at his shoes, considering her words. It was an inopportune time to notice just how thick his eyelashes were or how his open shirt collar showed the dark shadow of body hair.

He looked up, smiling slightly as he said, 'Don't be sorry, Beth. Allow them their little stories and fantasies. I'm sure the truth is far duller than anything they've come up with.'

Cheeky hound. Now her stare turned into a

glare and it was a moment or two before she warned herself not to show any emotion. Straightening her face and stitching a smile where the frown had been, she said nonchalantly, 'Guaranteed, for sure.'

A shrill beeping from the direction of the kitchen filtered through, telling her the timer on the oven was announcing her meal was cooked. Travis cocked his head. 'Do you need to see to something?' he asked mildly.

'It's fine. Just my evening meal,' she said dismissively, hoping he'd take the hint and leave, especially as she hadn't offered to refill his glass.

Instead he said, 'I thought I could smell something delicious. What are you having?' He sniffed the air.

'A casserole.' And when the black brows continued to silently question, she added, 'Pork with parsnip and apple.' At least she hoped that was what it tasted like.

He all but smacked his lips. 'Sounds good.' And still he sat there as though he had a perfect right to.

Beth found herself mentally squirming, remembering how he'd taken her and Harvey in and made them so welcome. But this was different, she told herself silently. It was. Totally different. And the fact that she had cooked enough for two days, meaning to have the rest tomorrow, was nothing to do with it. She drained her glass and stood up, which was a relief in itself. The edge of the tub had been distinctly uncomfortable to perch on. Still Travis made no effort to leave.

The silence was now screaming and, acknowledging he'd won, she said flatly, 'Have you eaten yet?'

'Me?' he said with an air of pliant meekness which didn't wash at all with Beth. 'No, I haven't, as it happens. It was a devil of a journey, traffic jams all the way, and I just wanted to get here.'

OK, OK, don't labour the point. 'I've enough for two if you'd like to stay,' she said shortly, her tone less than enthusiastic—to put it mildly.

Travis didn't appear to notice. 'Really? Great, I'd love to. If you're sure.' Black eyebrows quirked as he smiled.

Wretched man. Beth ignored the effect the devastating smile had on her insides, saying, 'It's a big cramped inside and there's no dining table, I'm afraid. You'll have to manage with a tray on your lap.' There was the little breakfast bar and that was where she usually ate, seated on one of the two stools the cottage boasted, but the tininess of the space would mean she'd be shoulder to shoulder with Travis and that was out of the question. She wouldn't be able to eat a thing.

'A tray is no problem,' he said easily.

A tray might not be, he most certainly was. As Travis went to stand up, Beth said hastily, 'No, you sit where you are and I'll call you when it's ready. The cottage is so tiny…' She took his glass. 'I'll bring you out another glass of wine.'

'Thanks.' He slanted a look at her under half closed lids, his voice still suspiciously acquiescent when he said, 'Sure I can't help? I feel guilty landing on you like this.'

You've done quite enough already. 'No, it's fine. I won't be a minute.' She smiled briskly and marched away.

Once inside the cottage, Beth stared down at Harvey who had followed her in. How on earth had she come to find herself in this position? One moment it had been just her and Harvey sitting in peaceful tranquillity and enjoying the summer evening. The next… She poured Travis another glass of wine and took it out to him before he took it into his head to ignore what she had said and follow her inside.

He was sitting with his legs outstretched and his eyes shut, his face lifted to the dying sunlight. He looked big and hard and as sexy as hell, and as she stared at him something like a bolt of electricity shot down to her toes, making them curl. She had to swallow twice before she could mutter, 'Here's your wine,' and she made very sure their hands didn't touch as she passed him the glass.

After scuttling back into the cottage, Beth stood for a moment at the kitchen sink with one hand pressed against her galloping heart. This was stupid. She had to get a grip. She shut her eyes tight and then opened them again, gazing blankly across the room.

After a moment or two she forced herself to start setting two trays with cutlery and napkins, annoyed to see her hands were trembling slightly. She breathed in and out deeply a few times, her mind racing. OK, so she was sexually attracted to Travis—she admitted it. She sighed with relief. She had been trying to fight the reality for the last three weeks and it wasn't the way to handle this. She had to be honest with herself.

She lifted the steaming casserole out of the oven and on to the small steel shelf at the side of the hob.

She was a grown woman of thirty years of age, she told herself. Not a simpering schoolgirl in the midst of a first crush. Sexual attraction was the same the world over and it didn't mean a thing if you brought your will to bear. Mind over matter, simple. She was not about to get involved in a casual relationship with any man—Prince Charming himself could walk in here and she wouldn't be tempted.

She had believed in Keith, utterly and totally, and if she could get it so monumentally wrong once there was no guarantee she couldn't do so again. And she wasn't prepared to take such a risk. That left the sensible option. If she didn't let herself become vulnerable then she couldn't be hurt. And the way not to be vulnerable was not to get close to a man.

She reached for the dish of thinly sliced layered potatoes on the second shelf of the oven and they sizzled at her, the butter and seasoning she'd sprinkled over them pleasantly aromatic. For once everything looked delicious.

She had several friends who could handle one-night stands and relationships with no strings attached perfectly well, but she knew she wasn't made that way. She'd had lots of other boyfriends, one or two quite serious, before Keith, but she had never fully committed in a physical sense because that certain undefinable something had been missing. Keith was the first man she had been to bed with and it looked as if he might be the last. She grimaced and began ladling the casserole on to the oven-warmed plates, swiftly followed by the golden-brown potatoes. But better that than being taken for a mug again.

'I must be able to do something?'

As the deep rich voice from the doorway

startled her, Beth almost dropped the dish of potatoes. Nerving herself, she glanced at Travis. It was the best bit of acting she had done for some time when she shrugged nonchalantly, her voice airy as she said, 'No, it's all under control. Go and sit down and I'll bring the trays through in a moment or two.'

'Let me take your glass and the rest of the wine at least.' He had moved into the kitchen before she could stop him, reaching across her for the bottle. The movement brought his shoulder brushing against her arm and suddenly the faint intoxicating smell of his aftershave was there on her senses, along with a quivering awareness of the height and breadth of the powerful male body.

Beth froze. She couldn't breathe. It was a huge relief when he strolled into the sitting room.

Idiot! She made herself continue to dish up the meal even as the little shivers radiating from every nerve and sinew made themselves felt. She was a twenty-four carat idiot. He wasn't going to pounce on her, for goodness' sake, or turn into a demented rapist or depraved pervert.

But then it wasn't any of those possibilities that was bothering her, a little voice in her head said nastily. It was more how she would react if he did try to kiss her that had got her all of a twitter.

She stared at the two full plates and then

breathed out slowly. Calm, girl, calm. You give him dinner—you owe him that at least—but then your debt is paid. Keep it nice and friendly but cool, a definite one-off. He'll get the message.

She picked up the plates and placed them on the trays, taking one and preparing to carry it through to Travis. An hour, two at the most, and then she could call a halt to the evening. After that she needn't see him again, apart from perhaps the odd glance and wave if he happened to pass the gate when she was in the garden.

She mentally nodded at the thought. Travis was the sort of man who would never be short of female companionship, that was for sure. Why, next week or the next or some time very soon she most likely would see a blonde, brunette or redhead sitting next to him as the car drove past. Perhaps even a succession as the months passed. And that was fine, just fine.

Her chin rose, her soft full mouth pulled itself tighter and her back straightened. And it was like that, with her head held high, that she took the tray through to him.

CHAPTER FOUR

'THAT WAS WONDERFUL.' Travis put down his knife and fork with the appearance of a man who was replete.

'I'm glad you enjoyed it,' Beth said primly. Actually she had been surprised by how good the food had tasted. For someone who normally managed to make boiling an egg a disaster, the meal had turned out very well. 'I haven't got anything like hazelnut pie or apple crumble, I'm afraid,' she added with a brief smile, 'but there's cheese and biscuits for dessert if you'd like some.' She might as well finish the meal properly.

'My favourite.' He grinned at her. 'And the hazelnut pie and apple crumble were both shop bought, by the way.'

Too cosy. Too intimate. Beth rose swiftly from the chair she had purposely made sure she sat in when Travis had taken the sofa, but as she reached for his plate he too stood up. 'Allow me,' he said firmly, taking her plate from her and walking through to the kitchen, where he dunked the plates in the washing-up bowl before she could protest.

She stood hovering in the doorway. The kitchen was too small for the two of them but she couldn't very well order him out. 'Please leave the washing-up; I'll do it later,' she said at last. 'Come and have another glass of wine.'

'Nearly finished.' It was a minute or two before he turned and then he didn't move away from the sink, leaning against it, arms folded, legs crossed as he surveyed her from intense grey eyes. 'Have you been abused? Sexually, I mean,' he asked with shocking matter-of-factness.

'What?' She couldn't believe her ears, her face flooding with hot colour. 'Of course not.'

'There's no "of course" about it. It happens.'

'Well, it hasn't to me.' She couldn't believe he had asked her such a thing. She wanted to die with embarrassment.

'Then why are you as jumpy as a cat on a hot tin roof if I'm anywhere within three feet of you?' he said coolly.

'I'm not.' She glared at him. 'Don't be silly.'

'I think you are.' He levered himself upright and took the couple of steps to reach her.

Beth brought every muscle into play and remained quite still and unflinching as she looked at him. 'Just because I came here for peace and quiet it doesn't mean I've got some huge problem,' she said with steely control, 'merely that I don't want to socialise with folk. That's not a crime, is it?'

'Not at all,' he said softly.

He wasn't touching her but he was so close she could almost feel the thud of his heartbeat and it took all of her will not to retreat. 'So, if you just move out of the way, I'll get the cheese and biscuits,' she finished icily.

'If you haven't been hurt sexually, then what is it?' he asked very quietly. 'Because there's something, isn't there? Something that's made you retreat from the human race. Or the male part of it. It isn't just work that's sent you here.'

She didn't know how to handle his gentle persistence. The seconds seemed to stretch on for an eternity before she could bring herself to say, 'Are you always like this? So...'

'Straightforward?' he interjected pleasantly.

'I was going to say offensive.'

'Always.' He didn't smile. 'So what is it?'

Beth knew her face was burning. 'Haven't you ever heard it's rude to invade someone else's privacy?' she asked tersely.

He ignored this. She got the feeling he always ignored anything he did not want to answer.

'What was his name?' he asked softly. 'This man who let you down?'

She stared at him as her mind raced. Useless to prevaricate—she could read in his eyes he wasn't going to let go of this. 'Keith.' Although it was hard, she made herself continue to look him straight in the face without dropping her gaze. 'His name was Keith, all right? He was my husband for a while until I discovered he had a common law wife and two children he'd forgotten to mention. In my eyes, if not legally, he was a bigamist.'

She saw him blink and knew she had shocked him. 'I'm sorry.' His voice was deep and sincere. 'I can't imagine how that must have made you feel.'

There was something in the hard male face that made her want to cry but she had cried enough tears to fill an ocean in the last months. To combat the weakness she deliberately made her voice flippant when she said, 'Pretty rough to start with but in the overall scheme of things it was just a little dropped stitch in life's rich tapestry. And, let's face it, it isn't many women who get to be the legal wife and the other woman at the same time. I feel sorry for Anna, actually. She didn't know about me either and she has two little children to consider. He was very clever, dividing his time between two households and keeping us both sweet. There might even have been other women on the side too; it wouldn't surprise me.'

'So you left him?' Travis asked quietly.

'Oh, yes. Like a shot. We're divorced now so it's all history,' she said evenly. 'Everything was made worse by the fact that my sister and I had recently lost our parents in an accident and I worked too hard to try and cope with it all. Bad mistake. So you see there is no deep mystery to my being in these parts. Not really. I just decided I wanted a nice long break before I join the rat race again, that's all.'

'What about the human race?'

'Pardon?' She frowned at him.

'When are you planning on joining the human race again? Letting down the drawbridge? Communicating? Having fun? Dating?' he said smoothly. 'Normal stuff.'

Her frown turned into a full scale glare. 'That's my business, surely,' she said frostily. Didn't he realise how devastating it had all been? Was the man without even the merest shred of understanding?

He held up his hands in mock surrender, stepping back a pace. 'OK, OK, don't get super-prickly again. I only wondered how long you intended to let him dominate your life and cast a shadow over your future. Months, years?'

'*What?*' Beth was flabbergasted. How *dared* he?

He eyed her expressionlessly. 'Well, what do you call it?' he asked coolly. 'The guy was obviously an out-and-out sleazeball who wasn't fit to draw breath; every generation throws up a few like him. They're dangerous, I give you that, but only before you recognise what they are. Afterwards, once they're back in the gutter where they belong, you get on with the rest of your life. Or else they win big time. Surely not an option?'

Beth couldn't remember being so mad for a long time. 'As easy as that, eh?' she said grimly. 'Well, silly old me for not realising the world is just a bowl of fat ripe cherries and the moon's really made of cheese. I'll be believing in Santa Clause next and the tooth fairy.'

He had the nerve to grin. 'Whatever turns you on.'

For the first time since she had been a little girl, Beth found herself stamping her foot. Within the warm circle of her family home she'd had the nickname Neddy because of her tendency to stamp up and down in temper. The brief lack of control was like a dash of icy water on the fire of her anger. Taking a deep breath, she said, 'I think you had better go.'

'Because I told you the truth?' he said lazily, not moving. 'You're big enough to take it, surely?'

She almost stamped again. Infuriating, arrogant *pig* of a man. 'The truth as Travis Black sees it,' she qualified curtly. 'Which doesn't necessarily make it the truth at all.'

'Think about what I've said and you'll find I'm right.' He wasn't smiling any more. 'You're too beautiful and warm and gutsy to shut yourself away, Beth, and, if you're not careful, the longer you leave it before you put a toe back in the water the harder it'll be to launch out and swim.'

'And if I don't want to swim again?' she said tightly. 'That's up to me, surely. I do have a mind of my own.'

'Believe me, I don't doubt it.' His voice was dry.

'Please go.' She turned and walked into the sitting room, wondering what she would do if he didn't follow her. He did.

As she opened the front door and stood aside for him to leave, he paused in front of her. 'I shall pick you up for Sunday lunch at twelve,' he said quietly. 'On the dot, OK?'

She looked at him in absolute amazement, too surprised to even feel outraged at his temerity. Finding her voice, she said, 'You are the last person in the world I'd have lunch with, Travis, so don't waste your time calling.'

'Twelve, on the dot.' He bent, kissing her swiftly with the lightest of kisses on her lips, before walking out of the cottage. The evening shadows swallowed him up and he didn't look back.

She didn't wait to see if he reached his car before she closed the door, leaning against it as she felt her legs threaten to let her down. Harvey was at her feet whining, and it was only when she stroked his coarse fur to reassure him she was all right that she realised how badly she was trembling.

It had been the briefest of kisses, barely a kiss at all, so why had it affected her so deeply? The silent room provided no answer. Not that she had expected it to.

After a minute or two she felt the strength to move away from the door, walking into the kitchen and surveying the remains of the casserole. 'A social nicety.' She said the words out loud as though that would help convince her how ridiculous she was being. That was all such a kiss was to a man like Travis. Something you did when you left a dinner party or something similar. A polite finale to the evening.

She put her hands to her hot face, her head whirling with so many thoughts and emotions she felt giddy. It didn't help that her lips were burning where his had touched or that for the short fleeting moment when his flesh had touched hers time had stood still. The smell, the feel, the sheer potency of him was still lingering and she didn't want it to. She didn't *want* to feel like this. She didn't want him to affect her at all.

She groaned, shaking her head at her weakness. He had called Keith dangerous, but Travis was in a league all of his own. What was she going to do?

She was still asking herself the same question when she crawled into bed that night, emotionally and mentally exhausted. Endless post mortems of every word spoken, every gesture, every nuance in Travis's voice had made her more confused than ever. But one thing was certain, she told herself as she lay in the warm darkness scented by the rambling roses outside her open window. She was *not* going to have Sunday lunch with him. She still could hardly believe she'd heard aright after the way the evening had gone. It was proof of how arrogant he was.

An owl hooted in the woods surrounding the cottage, the elemental sound comforting in a forever kind of way. In all the trauma and drama of recent months, the agonising pain she'd felt at losing her parents so unexpectedly and then the hurt and betrayal by Keith, this wood had gone on for generations. Some of the old oak trees had been here a century or two before she'd been born and would still be here when she was gone.

Beth pulled the thin linen sheet up round her ears and determinedly shut her eyes, the jumbled maelstrom of her thoughts quietening suddenly. She couldn't stop Travis coming here on Sunday morning but she could make sure she wasn't in. And that wasn't cowardice. It was simply hammering home the simple truth that she wanted nothing at all to do with him. *Nothing.*

In spite of her conviction she was doing the only thing possible in the circumstances and that was far better than having a shouting match on the doorstep, Beth couldn't help feeling inordinately guilty as she left the cottage at ten o'clock on Sunday morning. She had packed a picnic lunch for herself and Harvey and intended to spend the hot and sunny summer's day tramping the hills and valleys in the surrounding countryside. And she would think of nothing at all. All day.

She spent what should have been an idyllic day in the fresh air, returning home at twilight. The flowering grass beneath her feet was soft and shimmering in the evening light as the warm breeze ruffled it, the birds twittering as they prepared for darkness in the trees and bushes and a flock of sheep placid and silent in the fields below the cottage as she emerged close to the house. As she approached the garden gate eight large birds circled overhead in the last rays of the setting sun, the delicate pattern on their wings turning to purest gold where the light touched them. The beauty of the moment took Beth's breath away.

So why, when she'd had a perfectly lovely day with Harvey and everything was so peaceful and tranquil, should she be feeling so wretched? she asked herself, opening the gate. All day she had been fighting thoughts of Travis but no matter how she had tried to keep him at bay he'd insisted on forcing himself into the front of her mind.

And it wasn't as if she'd done anything wrong, not really. She had *told* him she wouldn't have lunch with him so if he had turned up expecting her to go out with him he only had himself to blame. She wasn't responsible for his stubbornness.

She was almost at the cottage door when she heard the approaching car in the lane outside the garden. Her heart plummeted, but telling herself she would have had to face him at some point in the future so it might as well be now, she turned and retraced her steps. When the car came into view she was standing holding Harvey's collar in the garden, unaware of how slender and defensive she looked in the shadowed night.

The car stopped, but at the same time as Travis extracted himself from the vehicle a pretty brunette slid out of the passenger seat. 'You must be Beth!' Before Travis could say a word the girl was walking over to the gate. 'I've heard all about you. I think it's terrific you've chosen to come and live all by yourself for a while and to hell with the rest of the world.'

Completely taken aback, Beth forced a smile. 'Thanks—I think,' she said, keeping her eyes from straying to the big male figure coming up behind the girl.

'I'm Sandra, Travis's sister, and I don't blame you at all for standing him up this lunchtime.' Sandra extended a hand to shake and, feeling a little stunned, Beth took it. 'I'd have done exactly the same thing if I'd been you.'

'Hello, Beth.' Travis's voice was very dry and as her gaze moved to him she saw the dark face was still and coolly imperturbable. She couldn't read a thing in the closed expression.

Answering Sandra but looking at Travis, Beth said a little shakily, 'I didn't stand him up. I told him I wasn't going to have lunch with him. I made it absolutely clear, in fact.'

'But he wouldn't take no for an answer?' Sandra nodded. 'That's my brother all over. The stories I could tell you. He's really bull-headed. When he gets the bit between his teeth—'

'You've introduced yourself to Beth, Sandra. Now it's time to go and sit in the car.' Travis's voice was soft and cool as it cut across his sister's chatter but there was no doubting it was an order and not a request.

Beth saw the other girl open her mouth as though to protest but when she glanced at her brother's face she must have thought better of it. 'See you again soon,' she dimpled at Beth before swinging round and depositing herself in the Mercedes, closing the door behind her.

Beth's stomach was churning but her face betrayed none of her agitation as she looked at Travis, trying desperately to ignore how good he looked. 'I did say I wasn't going to have lunch,' she repeated flatly. 'If you remember?'

'I remember. It went something along the lines of I would be the last person on earth you'd lunch with. Right?'

Flushing slightly, Beth said, 'Right. So you can't say I stood you up.' Her chin lifted defiantly.

'I didn't. Sandra did.' He smiled—a smile which didn't reach the piercing eyes. 'It was her interpretation of events, not mine. I was ninety-nine per cent sure you wouldn't be in when we called, as it happens. OK?'

She stared at him. He meant it, she could tell. 'So why call, then?' she asked bewilderedly. 'Why did you bother?'

'In hope of the one per cent,' he said softly. 'Good night, Beth.' He turned on his heel and walked away.

He had reached the car before she could force

herself to say, 'Travis? I'm sorry. Not that I didn't have lunch with you, because I don't want to have lunch with anyone, but that I've been so…' She didn't know how to put it.

He stood with his hand on the car door. In the shadowed night his eyes looked black and there was a small smile twisting his lips. 'Touchy?' he suggested very softly.

'Bitchy.' She swallowed hard. 'Because I'm not like that, not usually. At least I don't think I am. Although I know I've changed since the divorce, so perhaps this is the real new me. But I hope not.' She stopped abruptly. She was babbling; she would have known even if his face hadn't told her so. 'Anyway, I'm sorry,' she finished flatly. And she really was.

'How sorry?' he asked with silky intent.

'What?' Her brow wrinkled.

'How sorry are you?' he asked with magnificent blandness, his voice and manner betraying nothing but a kind of amiable forbearance. 'Sorry enough to share the odd meal with me when I'm in these parts without thinking I've some ulterior motive like ripping your clothes off and taking you to bed? You see, the truth of the matter is that sexually you're not my type, Beth, but I find you interesting as a person. And that's a compliment, incidentally,' he added pleasantly. 'There's few people, men or women, I find interesting.'

She was so shocked that automatic pilot clicked in. 'I see,' she said numbly. Charming, absolutely charming.

'We're close neighbours and in these parts that means you look out for each other, do the neighbourly thing,' Travis continued cheerfully. 'Get it? With you living such a solitary lifestyle I'd hate to think you were ill or had had an accident or any one of a number of things and no one knew.'

'I have a mobile phone,' she said tightly, 'and I talk to my sister all the time. And friends,' she added quickly so that he wouldn't think she was the ultimate sad case. Although it appeared he was thinking that already. All the time she'd had the idea he fancied her, he'd obviously been feeling sorry for her. She wanted to fall on the floor and have a full scale paddy.

'Of course you do,' he said soothingly, so soothingly she wanted to sock him on the jaw. 'But that's not like seeing someone in the flesh, is it?'

She couldn't help the shiver that trickled down her spine, even though she told herself Travis would feel even more sorry for her if he knew she was inventing double meanings for his innocent remarks. Her cheeks burning, she tried to pull herself together. 'I'm quite capable of looking after myself, so don't worry about me,' she said grimly. How dared he pity her? She didn't need anything from Travis Black.

'Nevertheless, I'd like to feel I could call by or you could call for me if the need arose. You understand? I think what I'm trying to say is that it would be good if we could be friends, Beth. OK?' He raised black eyebrows enquiringly.

She had never felt so insulted in her life. The thought was there even though she told herself she was being utterly unreasonable, not to mention contradictory. She hadn't wanted him to be interested in her, had she? Of course she hadn't. She'd been telling herself that since she had arrived in Shropshire. And he was offering platonic, no strings attached friendship. She ought to feel relieved. But she didn't feel relieved, she felt... Ooh, she didn't know *how* she felt, which was even more maddening.

Becoming aware he was waiting for an answer, she stitched a grimace on her face that just about passed for a smile, saying, 'Yes, of course, I understand. That's fine, just fine.'

'Good.' He had the audacity to smile a kind of 'there there, you'll be all right one day' smile. Or at least that was how she interpreted it and it made her blood boil. 'I'm glad we had the chance to clear the air. I'm going back tonight but how about a meal or something next time I'm around?'

In view of everything that had gone on she could hardly refuse. Gritting her teeth, she said brightly, 'Yes, OK.'

'Great.' He made a movement as though to open the car door but then seemed to change his mind. As he walked back to her Beth felt her stomach do a bungee jump that would have rivalled anything she'd seen on TV. 'See you soon then,' he said briskly, bending and doing the thing where he skimmed her lips again. A polite farewell. Sexless. Chummy.

At least it was clearly a social kiss of the lightest kind to him, Beth thought, trembling as she watched him return to the car and slide in it this time. A moment later it drove off, Sandra waving from the passenger window. Unfortunately it was not that simple where she was concerned. But then, she reminded herself bitterly, Travis didn't fancy *her* apparently. She did nothing for him at all. Whereas she...

She fancied the pants off him.

Purely a physical thing, she assured herself hastily in the next moment, and as such easily controlled. No emotions involved after all, just raging hormones. Which was perhaps understandable in a way. She'd had an active sex life with Keith and then it had suddenly stopped dead. It was only natural that now she was beginning to feel better again her body would remind her that she was a flesh and blood woman. While she had been working all hours and coping with the loss of her parents and the agony of Keith's betrayal such things had been smothered. Now, rested and in lovely tranquil surroundings with no mad whirl to exhaust her and make her mentally and physically drained, things were different. The old libido was up and running once more.

She turned from the gate, walking to the front door where Harvey was lying waiting for her. The big dog stood up at her approach, tongue lolling and tail wagging as he anticipated his evening meal. Beth smiled at him, bending and patting the coarse fur as she thought, this isn't really to do with Travis Black—it could be any man. He just happens to be the one around at the moment, the one that's awoken that side of life once more.

She told herself the same thing several times throughout the evening before she went to bed. She was still telling herself it as she drifted off to sleep. And not once did she allow herself to question why it was so important that Travis was relegated to the rank of ordinary males.

CHAPTER FIVE

THE NEXT WEEK crawled by with surprising slowness, probably, Beth admitted, because she just couldn't stop thinking about Travis. Where he was, what he was doing and with whom. It aggravated her to distraction but although she tried the therapy of endless walks with Harvey, cleaning the cottage from top to bottom—something which hadn't happened for some time, she discovered, when she tackled the backs of the kitchen cupboards—and writing copious letters to all and sundry telling them how much better she was feeling, nothing took her mind off him for long.

As the weekend approached she found herself counting the hours and was genuinely appalled at her weakness, especially as she couldn't discern whether the overriding feeling which had her heart missing a beat now and again was one of excitement or nervousness. Whatever, it didn't make for restful sleep or tranquil days.

Which made her angry and even more disturbed.

On Friday morning when her mobile rang just as she'd sat down in the tiny back garden with Harvey, a cup of coffee and a plateful of wickedly delicious chocolate biscuits at her side, her heart did a mad gallop before she realised Travis didn't have her number so it couldn't be him making an arrangement about the weekend. Shaking her head at herself, she answered the call.

'Beth?' Catherine's voice was all bubbly. 'Guess what? Michael's mother has offered to have James for a couple of days so we can have a loved-up weekend by ourselves, and Michael's booked a hotel on the outskirts of Shropshire so we can call in and take you out for a meal for a few hours. What do you think? Oh, Neddy, I can't wait to see you. It seems like ages.'

Catherine's use of the old nickname told Beth her sister meant what she said. Catherine only ever used it when she was feeling particularly sentimental.

'But if it's supposed to be a weekend for you and Michael, won't he mind?' she prevaricated. She got on well with her brother-in-law, who was a true salt of the earth type, but she didn't want to take advantage of his good nature, something Catherine was prone to do on occasion.

'Darling, it was Michael who suggested it and

booked the hotel, I promise. He knows how much I've been missing you. And it'll only be for a few hours. I'll make sure I reward him handsomely for his sacrifice, I assure you.' She giggled. 'So, how about we call for you tomorrow evening? Say about sixish? You can tell me all the Aga-saga gossip. It'll be lovely.'

'Cath, I don't see a soul and that's what I love, but do come if you're sure you can spare some time out of your precious weekend. It would be lovely to see you, but only if you're sure.'

'Totally. And I'll bring the latest photos of James. You won't believe how much he's changed in a month. See you tomorrow, then. Love you, little sis. Very much.'

'Love you too and can't wait to see you.'

Beth finished the call and put the phone down, picking up the fragrant mug of hazelnut coffee and licking the creamy froth with the tip of her tongue. She hoped Travis called by before Sunday so she could make it clear she was going out for the evening. That would teach him to suggest she was the equivalent of a friendless little orphan Annie.

And then she sat sharply upright, cross with herself for caring what he might or might not think. For goodness' sake, what was the matter with her? She was letting him monopolise her thoughts in a way that had never happened before.

She had to get a grip! She was turning into one neurotic female.

She drank the coffee and shared the biscuits with a slavering Harvey before going for a long walk, and once home again worked in the front garden for the rest of the day. After checking it was all right with the owner of the cottage via John Turner, she had decided to create a border of flowers in the somewhat sterile frontage and had bought several trays of brightly coloured primulas, Michaelmas daisies, delphiniums and other hardy perennials from a local garden centre. It might not be financially sensible, but she felt the cottage was giving her so much that she wanted to put a little back.

She worked on until a soft-scented twilight fell, refusing to acknowledge that for the last few hours she had had one ear cocked for the sound of a car approaching. At last, when it was too dark to see, she retired to the cottage with a somewhat crestfallen Harvey who had been ad-monished more than once for happily digging in the freshly overturned earth, thereby scattering flowers in all directions.

Perhaps Travis wasn't going to come this weekend, after all. As she made supper, Beth told herself she didn't care one way or the other. Maybe work commitments or even things of a more personal nature were keeping him in Bristol. He was a very attractive man; there were bound to be plenty of women who would have their eye on him.

She didn't know why she felt so disgruntled and irritable as she got ready for bed, or why she lay awake for a good couple of hours before she drifted off into a troubled sleep full of complicated tangled dreams and shadowed images. Or perhaps it was just that she didn't want to know. Whatever—self-examination was not an option.

Catherine and Michael arrived on the dot of six o'clock the next day. Harvey was delighted to see his old friends and gave them an ecstatic welcome, and Beth's sister and her husband declared themselves in love with the cottage and its position. With Shropshire in general, in fact.

'I can see why you took this place,' Catherine said once Beth had shown them round and then settled the pair of them on the sofa with a cold drink. 'It's so peaceful. Mind, I don't think I'd want to be here all by myself in the winter.'

'I'll be back in London by then.' Beth smiled as she spoke, although her heart gave a funny little lurch at the thought of leaving. Already the cottage seemed like home.

Catherine nodded. 'And what about him—your knight in shining armour?' she asked archly.

'Have you seen any more of him since he rescued you from the brink of disaster?'

'Hardly a disaster.' Beth laughed and hoped her sister didn't notice it was forced. She had mentioned her somewhat shaky start in Shropshire but glossed over Travis's part in it as much as possible, although she might have known Catherine would seize on the fact that an attractive unattached man was in the immediate vicinity. Her sister had already made it plain more than once that the best way to forget Keith was to meet someone else. In fact they'd nearly argued about it before she had left London. Eventually they'd agreed to differ.

'So, have you seen him again?' Catherine persisted, ignoring the pointed glance Michael gave her which suggested she was being too nosy. 'Travis, wasn't it?'

Beth nodded. 'Once or twice in passing,' she said casually, adding, 'and where are those photos of James you mentioned? I'm dying to see them.'

The diversion worked as Beth had known it would. Catherine worshipped the ground her baby toddled on and had already confessed to phoning Michael's mother six times since they had left London—just to make sure everything was all right.

Beth oohed and ahhed over the pictures of her nephew enough to satisfy even Catherine, but while she looked at the bright-eyed little boy and made all the right noises, she was reflecting that it was extremely fortuitous that Travis hadn't turned up. Although it would have been satisfying to show him she was far removed from the hermit he'd suggested she was, Catherine might get the wrong idea. And once Catherine was on a mission wild horses wouldn't deflect her from her purpose.

Michael had booked a table at the hotel he and Catherine were staying at, which was half an hour's drive from the cottage. Although Beth felt slightly guilty at the miles involved in their seeing her, she told herself it was Michael's decision and one which she secretly welcomed. There was no chance of running into Travis there if he did decide to arrive late, whereas the village pub might have presented a danger.

She had already spent some time getting ready before Catherine and Michael arrived, determined to present an upbeat, together image to her sister. She knew Catherine worried about her and so she had taken special care with her appearance, choosing a sleeveless wispy chiffon dress in a deep blue shade which emphasised the blue in her eyes, dressing it up with a wide funky se-quinned belt and fragile ankle-strap sandals. It had actually felt good to apply make-up and bother with her hair for the first time in ages.

Having had a break from doing it every day now made it a pleasure.

So when, at just gone seven, Michael suggested they make a move, Beth was ready to go, after quickly collecting her bag and short-sleeved cotton cardigan from the bedroom.

After telling Harvey to be 'on guard', an instruction the big dog understood to mean he wouldn't be accompanying her, Beth led the way to the front door. Catherine had cheekily enquired if she was sure she'd got her key as Beth opened the door and, smiling, Beth had been about to reply in kind. Her mouth failed to form the words.

Her eyes widening, she stared aghast at Travis, who slowly lowered the hand with which he'd been about to knock. He looked good. More than good. Sensational.

'Hello, Beth.'

It was soft but the low murmur was enough to bring Catherine nudging up behind her, her sister's voice holding a bright note as she said eagerly, 'Well, hello there. We didn't hear you, did we, Beth? I'm Catherine, Beth's sister, by the way. And, as it doesn't look as though she's going to introduce anyone, this—' she waved a hand at Michael, who was out of Travis's line of vision, having had the good manners not to rush to the doorway and stare as his wife was doing '—is my husband, Michael.'

Recovering herself, Beth took a deep breath. 'I'm sorry,' she said evenly, 'you startled me, that's all. Beth, Michael, this is Travis Black. I think I mentioned that he helped out the first night I was here.'

'When you locked yourself out and he took you home for bed and breakfast?' Catherine said outrageously. 'Course I remember.'

'Don't forget a very good dinner was included too.' Travis smiled at Catherine over Beth's shoulder and she was forced to stand back so Catherine could take the hand Travis was holding out. 'Nice to meet you, Catherine.'

As Catherine dimpled at Travis, Michael came forward and shook hands too so that Beth found herself edged further back into the room. Another minute and she'd be in the back garden!

'You very nearly missed us,' Catherine said chirpily. 'We have come to take Beth out to dinner. Have you eaten yet, Mr. Black?' she added archly.

'Travis, please. And no, I haven't eaten,' Travis said quietly. 'In fact, I was going to ask Beth the same question and suggest she might like to join me. But of course as you're visiting…' He paused delicately. Beth could have kicked him.

'Oh, no, no, you must join us,' Catherine protested quickly as Travis made to step backwards. 'We insist, don't we, Michael? We've booked a table at the hotel we're staying at, The Larches. Do you know it? I understand the food's wonderful.'

Travis nodded, his keen grey eyes passing the couple in front of him and focusing on Beth's tight face. 'Perhaps Beth would prefer to have you all to herself,' he said silkily. 'I'm sure you two must have plenty to catch up on.'

'Not at all.' Catherine swung round, took in Beth's wooden expression and turned to face Travis again. 'We talk on the phone nearly every day for hours,' she said airily, 'and we'd love to say thank you for looking after her so well when the whole incident could have turned out so badly.'

They were talking about her as though she'd suddenly gone blind, deaf and dumb. Beth stirred herself. 'Of course you must come if you haven't eaten,' she said sweetly to Travis, knowing full well it was all decided anyway. A ten ton truck wouldn't stand in the way of Catherine when she'd made up her mind about something. 'I wouldn't dream of seeing a friend starve when the solution is so simple.'

Travis's mouth curled in a smile that was so sexy Beth was sure he must have practised for hours in front of a mirror to get such a devastating result. 'Then thanks, I'd love to,' he said easily. He turned to Catherine. 'How about Beth and I follow you and Michael? It'll save you having to come all the way back here after the meal.'

'Well, if you're sure…' Catherine beamed at him.

'Quite sure.' He virtually beamed back.

Great. Beth wished she was two years old so she could indulge in a stress-relieving tantrum. But she wasn't a child and neither was Travis. He was a man and an all male one at that. Her mouth was dry and she had to swallow twice before she could say, 'Now that's settled, perhaps we ought to go if the table's booked for eight?'

'Absolutely. This is our first weekend by ourselves since our little boy was born, you know. Michael's mother is looking after him…' As Catherine took Travis's arm and continued to prattle away as they walked down the garden path, Michael just had time to mouth a silent 'sorry' to Beth before Travis disentangled himself and opened the garden gate for everyone to pass through. The good manners didn't cut any ice with Beth.

She was acutely conscious of the height and breadth of him as she brushed by, the dark trousers and white shirt he was wearing emphasising the leanness of his hips and the width of his powerful shoulders. She was also aware of the delicious tang of expensive aftershave on clean male skin, and felt there was some excuse for the fact she was finding it difficult to breathe. There was something about Travis that was broodingly tough and sensual, and yet there was a warmth, a fascinatingly gentle side to the hard masculinity that was compelling.

Animal attraction. A base kind of lust. She used the words deliberately. One caused the other. Simple. It was what made the world go round in the animal kingdom and it spilled over into the human population too. Keith had had that chemistry too, in a different kind of way to Travis, but it had been there nonetheless. Women would fall for such men regardless of whether they were free or involved with someone else, and the man barely had to lift his little finger. It was dangerous, with a high chance of disaster for the woman concerned, but it was a fact that some men only had to smile for the female sex to go down like ninepins. But not her. Never again.

Beth was so engrossed in her thoughts that she didn't notice Travis's car until she was almost standing by it, and even then it was more Catherine's frankly awed voice that brought her attention to the magnificent sports car. 'Wow, this must have cost you a fortune.' Catherine was nothing if not direct and to the point. 'Michael would die for one of these, wouldn't you, Mike? Every red-blooded man's dream and all that.'

As Michael dutifully agreed, Beth glanced at the

beautiful lines of the sleek Aston Martin crouched beside Catherine and Michael's stout family car. 'This is not your usual car,' she said accusingly as Travis opened the passenger door for her.

Travis studied her with the thoughtful look he seemed to keep for her. A 'here-we-go-again' look that suggested extreme patience and forbearance, Beth thought irritably.

'I have the Estate for when the dogs travel with me and this for when they don't,' he said mildly. 'Due to pressure of business, I didn't get away until late today and I have to get back tomorrow afternoon. It wasn't worth bringing them when they'll be perfectly OK with my housekeeper in Bristol.'

He had a Mercedes and an Aston Martin, the gorgeous house she'd seen that first night as well as another home complete with housekeeper. How much did industrial design pay these days, for goodness' sake? Beth slid into the leather interior.

Immediately he joined her Beth wished she had insisted they travel with Catherine and Michael. It would have made her look ridiculous, of course, as well as ungracious and selfish considering it would have meant Michael having to drive all the way back to the cottage to drop her off, but it would have been *so* worth it. As it was, she was trapped in this wildly sexy car with Travis so close she was in danger of hyperventilating.

She sat as stiff as a board as he expertly manoeuvred the powerful car to face the direction in which they were heading, her pulse racing. On the perimeter of her vision she was aware of strong male hands on the steering wheel and the way his trousers had pulled tight over hard thighs. It was disconcerting. The word mocked her with its feebleness.

As they began to follow the other car along the lane Travis settled more comfortably into his seat and Beth felt the action in every cell of her body. She swallowed to combat her dry mouth, pretending to look out of the side window as though she had never seen the view before.

'Your sister isn't much like you,' Travis observed coolly.

Beth looked at him out of the corner of her eye and saw he was perfectly relaxed and laid-back. The resentment she felt enabled her to say flatly, 'Actually, people have always said how alike we are. Catherine's only a couple of years older than me and there were times we were mistaken for twins when we were younger. Old aunties and uncles were forever getting us mixed up.'

'I wasn't referring to your physical appearance.'

'Oh, no?' Somehow she felt she came off unfavourably in the comparison. She didn't want to ask and give him the satisfaction of needling her, but she couldn't resist saying, 'What exactly were you referring to, then?'

He shrugged, considering his words for a moment before he murmured, 'She's friendly, bouncy, forever rushing in where angels fear to tread, I would imagine.'

Beth stared at the hard square jaw. There was a five o'clock shadow in evidence and the stubble was strong and dark. Beth didn't know why it made her stomach lurch but it did. Stiffly, she said, 'You make her sound like a cocker spaniel.'

He gave a crooked smile. 'Unintentional, I assure you.'

She knew she shouldn't ask—it was the craziest thing to do—so it was with some alarm she heard herself say, 'So if Catherine is your average cocker spaniel, how do you see me?'

'Quite differently.'

She wasn't sure if she had imagined the smoky warmth in his voice but it made her tremble anyway. She was overwhelmingly grateful he had to concentrate on the road ahead and wouldn't notice. Forcing a jaunty note into her voice, she said, 'Does that put me more in the category of a sedate collie or golden retriever? Something along those lines?'

Now he actually chuckled as he said, 'I wouldn't dream of comparing you to a dog, Beth.'

His lazy amusement caused a fresh riot of sensation in her traitorous body. She took in a long silent pull of air through her nostrils. 'But you admire Catherine's perkiness?' She kept her voice light, as though she didn't care one way or the other. Which she didn't, she assured herself silently.

'It takes all sorts to make the world go round.'

Undoubtedly, but that was hardly an answer. She sneaked a glance at the rugged profile from under her lashes. His smile was just a twitch this time but it told Beth he had noticed. She snapped her head to the front again at once.

Wretched man. She squirmed in her seat and then stopped herself immediately. Cool and collected, that was how she had to be to deal with Travis Black. She couldn't let him get under her skin. Deciding to change the subject entirely, she said primly, 'You are obviously very busy at work at the moment. I'm surprise you decided to come up this weekend.'

'Are you?' Grey eyes flashed over her face for a moment before his attention returned to the windscreen.

She waited for him to say more and when he didn't felt herself getting tenser and tenser. After a few electric minutes had quivered by, she broke the taut silence again, saying, 'Who exactly do you work for in Bristol?'

'Black Enterprises.'

'Black Enterprises? That's a coincidence, isn't it, the firm having the same name as...' She stopped. 'You have your own business,' she said lamely. Of course he did.

'That I do.' They had reached the main road now and as he turned his head and leant forward slightly at the junction she saw his hair had a small kink to it where it rested on his shirt collar. It was thick hair, virile, glowing with health.

Tearing her eyes away, she said weakly, 'Is it a family concern? I mean, did your father start it?'

He shook his head. 'No. My father died when I was ten years old and my mother married again when I was eighteen. I don't get on with her husband but, as I was going away to university, we were spared each other's company. They emigrated to New Zealand shortly afterwards and took my sister with them, but as soon as she was able she returned to England. By then my business was doing well and I was able to offer her a job.'

'So you looked after her?' She didn't like the fact that she was finding this glimpse into his life so fascinating but she couldn't help it.

Travis's mouth quirked. 'If Sandra heard you say that she would hit the roof. No, I didn't exactly look after her—we're too alike to let anyone do that—but she did work for me for a time before she took herself off to your neck of the woods, London. She's the PA to a clothing manufacturing magnate now and loves every minute.'

Beth nodded. 'She seemed feisty.'

'Oh, she is, Beth. Very feisty,' he said drily. 'And a total career woman.'

Once before she'd got the impression he didn't approve of his sister's lifestyle and it was stronger now. Or perhaps it was the fact that his sister was competing in what was still a male-dominated world and doing very nicely that bothered him? Maybe he was a male chauvinist at heart? The type of man who liked his women to know 'their' place? And certainly she, as an architect, wouldn't suit. Perhaps that was why he didn't fancy her as a woman? She turned her head to look out of the window.

She hadn't realised just how much his statement the last time they had seen each other had bothered her until this moment but, galling as it was to admit to herself, she'd let it get under her skin. Which was daft. His opinion of her didn't matter.

'A conversation with you is like walking blindfold in a minefield.'

Travis's voice was soft and for a moment his words didn't sink in. When they did, her eyes shot to meet his. They had just stopped behind Catherine and Michael at some traffic lights which meant he could give her his full attention, the grey eyes laser-like on hers. 'I don't have the faintest idea what you're talking about,' Beth said sharply.

'I'm talking about the way you were frowning out of the window just then.' The black eyebrows rose mockingly.

'I wasn't.' She straightened her face but it was too late.

'I don't like to be rude, but your face would have done credit to Queen Victoria,' he said pleasantly. 'What was it exactly that you objected to?'

Gritting her teeth in exasperation, Beth prevaricated with half the truth. 'I don't see why you should object to your sister following her own way of life,' she said tightly, 'or wanting a career. This is the twenty-first century, after all.'

'I don't.' He seemed surprised she'd thought so. 'Merely that she fails to exercise her considerable number of brain cells when it comes to her health by burning the candle at both ends. She's collapsed twice already in the last eighteen months. Burnt out. I don't want there to be a third time.'

'Oh.' She sat back in her seat a little, somewhat nonplussed. Then she rallied to say, 'But it's her life and if she's happy—'

'She is not happy,' Travis interrupted, just as the lights changed and his eyes returned to the road ahead. 'She made the mistake of dumping the love of her life before she left for London, thinking she couldn't have him and the career she wanted. She was wrong. You can have it all. You just have to work a little harder to make it happen.'

Beth immediately felt terribly sorry for Sandra. 'Poor thing,' she said in a tone which she hoped conveyed how hard she thought he was being. 'That's awful.'

'It was pretty awful for the guy concerned too,' Travis said shortly. 'Who happens to be a friend of mine.'

'Really?' Beth hadn't realised how many of Catherine's genes she shared, but she knew her sister would be proud of her if she could hear her now. 'In that case, couldn't you get the two of them back together? Try a little matchmaking?'

Travis shook his head. 'It took Sandra too long to come to her senses and by then Colin had married someone else.'

Beth was horrified. 'But if Sandra was the love of his life?'

'I said he was the love of *her* life—there's a difference,' Travis said softly. 'I don't know how Colin felt in the end. Maybe Sandra was just one of any number of women he could have been happy with. Maybe his wife is the love of his life. I don't know; we've never discussed it.'

'So…' Beth was feeling her way here. Groping in the dark. 'Do you believe people can meet and be happy with various other people but that there is only one person who is truly the love of their life?'

'Exactly,' he said, his voice cool. He didn't look at her as he continued, 'And you're damn lucky if you find them. Few do. And you're even luckier if they love you back in the same way. It happens but it's rare.'

She stared at him as the green countryside outside the car window flashed by. The evening was mellow and bathed in sunlight but the tranquillity was all outside the car. 'But that's a terribly jaundiced way of looking at relationships,' she said, ignoring the fact that in latter months she had been even more cynical about life and love. 'That means that most people are never truly happy, or at least not as happy as they could be.'

'Hence the divorce rate. And don't forget millions of couples live together for years and break up without getting married. In our grandparents' time you stayed together come what may and made the best of a bad job; people don't have to do that these days. How many friends of yours are on their second, third, even fourth serious relationship? They're all searching for that elusive thing they know is out there but have little chance of finding.'

Beth was appalled. There was no doubt he meant every word he was saying. After a moment or two she said, 'The world's a sad place according to you, then.'

'The world *can* be a sad place,' he corrected evenly. 'If you tie up with the wrong person, if you don't recognise the right one or they don't feel the same, but for those that hit the jackpot it's heaven on earth. My parents loved each other like that and my mother went for second best when she married again. Perhaps she was lonely or afraid of growing old by herself, I don't know, but she would have done better to remain single. She's been more unhappy married to my stepfather than she could have been living alone.'

'So if you never meet anyone you know is the love of your life you'll stay single for ever?' she said slowly.

'How do you know I haven't met her?' he asked very softly after a considerable number of seconds had ticked by.

'Because you'd be married and you aren't, are you?'

'No, I'm not.' He smiled. 'But that's because she didn't feel the same.'

Beth felt as though someone had punched her in the solar plexus. Which was as shocking—more shocking—than their conversation. Why should she care if Travis had been madly in love with someone he knew was the love of his life and who still held his heart, by the sound of it?

She didn't—she didn't care—she told herself in the next second. Not a personal kind of caring anyway. She just felt sorry for him, for anyone in that position. After the hurt and disillusionment she'd felt when her marriage broke up so suddenly she could feel for someone who was suffering, that was all. It was a horrible position to be in whoever you were.

She cleared her throat. 'I'm sorry,' she said quietly.

He shrugged. They drove on a good few miles before he said very softly, 'Was your husband the love of your life, Beth? Is that why you married him?'

'What?' She turned her head to look at him so quickly her neck cricked.

'Your husband,' he persisted gently. 'Was he the love of your life or just one of many men you could have been happy enough with if things had turned out differently?'

She wanted to tell him to mind his own business, but after he had been so open with her, she couldn't. He turned for a moment, his eyes meeting hers and then looked back to the road ahead. The car sped on, eating up the miles with consummate ease.

Her mind whirling, she tried to dredge up a reply. How could she answer such a question? She had felt her world had come crashing down about her ears when Anna had talked to her that day, had vowed never to put her trust in a member of the male species again, but… As her brain stopped scrambling her eyes widened. She'd survived. And it was as much the sudden loss of her parents that had caused her to overwork to forget as the breakdown of her marriage. What did that mean? She swallowed hard. 'I don't know,' she said after a full minute had passed. 'I don't know if Keith was the love of my life.'

'You don't know? Is that the truth or a way of telling me to shut up?' he said steadily, after one swift glance.

'It's the truth,' she said shakily. 'How can I know that?'

'Then he wasn't.'

It was so definite, so authoritative that immediately Beth rebelled. 'You can't say that,' she protested hotly. 'You don't know how I felt, how I feel.'

'That's true, but what I do know is that if he'd been the one you would have known. You'd know now.'

She didn't believe this! How dared he decide for her? 'I don't accept that,' she said vehemently.

'Is there a raw wound in your heart you know will never close unless you get back with this guy?' His voice was matter-of-fact, cool even. 'Something you tell yourself you'll have to learn to live with but which hurts like hell every minute?'

She couldn't honestly say there was but she wasn't going to give him fresh ammunition for his argument by admitting it. 'I'm not prepared to discuss this any further.'

'That's an answer in itself and it proves I'm right,' he said with what Beth considered immense arrogance. 'And you should be counting yourself lucky. From the little you've told me, your ex was an out-and-out jerk who isn't fit to draw breath. Let someone else put up with what he dishes out; you don't have to any more. You're free of him, free to make a new life.'

'That doesn't help Anna and their children,' she said self-righteously in an attempt to make him feel guilty. It didn't work. She hadn't really expected it to.

'It's up to her if she goes or stays. She had a choice, same as you did. And don't give me any flannel about her being trapped because of the kids,' he added, when Beth opened her mouth to do that very thing. 'Anyone with a grain of common sense would see they'd be far better off without a serial adulterer for a father who will most likely mess their minds up as badly as he seems to have messed up their mother's.'

She stared at him. 'I don't think I've ever met such an opinionated man as you,' she said with as much disdain as she could muster. 'You really do take the biscuit.'

All she had in answer was a grin. 'Considering the conversation we've just had, I'll count myself fortunate that's the most you've called me,' he said cheerfully, pulling up behind Michael and Catherine to let an old lady with what looked like dozens of little poodles on pink and blue leads cross the road. They took ages, absolutely ages.

He turned his head to face her and Beth met his eyes. She saw the genuine amusement there, the rugged face alight with a self-disparaging humour that was beguiling.

Dynamite. Even as she thought it, their shared glance deepened and held. She found she couldn't look away and she couldn't fathom why but all her nerve-endings were singing and alive, her body tingling. And Travis wasn't smiling any more. She couldn't put a name to the expression on his face.

How long the moment lasted she wasn't sure—it could have been seconds or hours given the way she was feeling—but then as the road ahead cleared he turned his head and broke the hold and the powerful car leapt forward.

Beth sat absolutely still and quiet, every cell of her body reeling. What had just happened? she asked herself silently. She didn't know. Whatever, it was the equivalent of being run over by a steamroller.

She discovered she had been holding her breath and forced herself to regulate her breathing and relax the hands which, unbeknown to her, had curled themselves into fists.

Dynamite, she repeated in her head. That was what he was. As dangerous as dynamite. And she didn't even like getting too close to fireworks! She groaned inwardly. But, regardless of how physically attracted she was to him—and that was all this was, physical attraction—he didn't fancy her, so that was all right. She was safe. It took two to tango.

She continued to breathe evenly and deeply and within a few minutes her body was behaving itself, but even though she was sitting straight she felt as limp as a wet rag. Ridiculous, but that one look had her feeling as shy as if they had just made love. Shyer.

Please, God, don't let him have guessed I fancy him, she prayed frantically throughout the rest of the journey. Not when he's made it absolutely clear I could be a mannequin in a clothes shop as far as he's concerned. She didn't apologise for the exaggeration, feeling it justified in the circumstances. She would die if he knew, she really would, and she still had another five or so months at the cottage to get through. Even though he only visited his second home in Shropshire now and again, she'd be a nervous wreck if she had to think about avoiding him. She'd be on tenterhooks every weekend, waiting to see if he was around.

As Travis followed Michael and Catherine into the car park of what looked to be a very nice country hotel some time later Beth realised they'd arrived. She didn't know if she was relieved or not. Although it would be good to remove herself from the intimacy of the car and join Catherine and Michael, she was worried how her sister would behave throughout the evening. Catherine seemed determined to link her and Travis together just because he had helped her that first night.

'You're tense. Don't be.' As Travis brought the car to a halt he reached out and placed a hand over hers, which were again clenched tightly in her lap. 'I know the score, OK? You intend to stay very firmly in that ivory tower you've built about yourself and repel invaders. And that's fine if that's what you want.' He paused. '*Is* it what you want, Beth?'

Beth glanced at the dark face. She didn't know what she wanted. In fact, she'd never felt more muddled in her life. And it was all *his* fault. Him and his flipping theories on this and that. She wished she had never met Travis Black.

'You're frowning again,' he said mildly, as though he didn't care but he didn't remove his hand from over hers.

Why did it matter to him what she wanted? Beth asked herself. She didn't even stir his body let alone his heart. Whereas his hand on hers, the feel of his warm firm flesh, was causing her heart to bump along like a car in the wrong gear. But then everything about this evening was wrong—everything. If it had been just the two of them…

The thought and the warm sensation in the most intimate part of her that accompanied it was enough to cause her to jerk her hands away from under his and say tightly, 'What do you expect me to do when you come out with such silly statements? I'm not in an ivory tower, as it happens, I'm very much in the world again, but I'm living life on my terms and I intend to go on doing so. I've got a mind and I intend to use it.'

'I'm glad to hear it.' He leant back in his seat and surveyed her with narrowed eyes. 'I like a positive approach.'

Beth stared at him. There was a look on his face she couldn't quite fathom.

'So what are those terms?' he asked just as Catherine and Michael left their car and began walking towards them. Before she could reply he wound down his window and said to her sister, who had paused by his door, 'We won't be a minute. You go in and we'll join you in a moment.'

'Oh, all right.' Catherine looked taken aback but pleased and Beth inwardly groaned. Now her sister would be thinking all sorts of things and galloping off down the wrong road entirely.

'So?' Travis had turned back to her again. 'The rules of engagement? Feel free to elucidate, Beth.'

She wished she hadn't started this. She breathed in the delicious warmth and smell of him and re-iterated silently for the hundredth time that she should never have got into the car. She shrugged as nonchalantly as she could. 'Why should you want to know?' she said a little breathlessly, hearing herself with a touch of annoyance. Breathlessness was not an option round Travis. More firmly, she added, 'You said you don't fancy me and just want to be friends. Surely the rules of engagement, as you call them, don't interest you?'

'Ah, but I lied, Beth.' The grey gaze didn't waver.

'What?' Utterly taken aback, she stared at him.

'I lied.' A small smile lifted the corners of Travis's mouth and she knew she was sitting with her mouth open and must look gormless, but she was so surprised she couldn't help it. 'You know, tell an untruth? Fabricate? Falsify?'

'I know what a lie means,' she snapped, but not as curtly as she would have liked. It was hard to be furious when exciting little shivers were racing up and down her spine. 'Why?' she managed eventually when he didn't say anything. 'Why did you lie about…?'

'Finding you sexually attractive?' His voice lingered over the third word and the shivers increased. 'Because you seemed to be panicking and I didn't like the idea I was driving you out of your house. We got off on the wrong foot, I know that, but taking yourself off for hours tramping the forest with Harvey to avoid me seemed a trifle…desperate. But I only half lied,' he added quietly.

'Half?' she said warily. 'What do you mean?'

'I said I found you interesting as a person and I do.' He leant forward and every nerve in her body responded. 'I'm not a spotty teenager, Beth, whose only idea of a relationship is to find out what the birds and bees are about. I've had women, I don't deny it, and I would be lying if I said I didn't want to take you to bed. But not now, not before you're ready. I'd like to get to know you and for you to know me, and then, if you want things to progress…'

'And if I don't?' She was trembling so much she knew he could see it. 'What happens then?'

'Then we kiss and walk away.' His gaze didn't vacillate.

She ran a shaky hand across her face. 'I'm…

I'm not ready for a relationship, however slow you're willing to take it. It's too soon after… everything that's happened.'

He had slightly adjusted his position as she spoke and she knew he was going to kiss her. Something had shifted and changed in the last minute or so, something indefinable but nevertheless very potent. She stared into his deep grey eyes and then his mouth touched hers but this was no light caress like before. This time his lips were warm and searching, intoxicating. He made no move to hold her or draw her into him as the kiss deepened—he didn't have to. Already a burning heat was flowing along every vein and she felt heady with the thrill of it.

She had known he would be able to kiss like this. The knowledge had been there from the first time she had seen him and even the brief fleeting caress he'd dropped so casually on her lips before had confirmed it. Sensual expertise was evident in every movement and action he made, the way he carried himself, his lazy self-assurance and effortless control.

And then in the next moment he lifted his head and settled back in his own seat, leaving her so bereft for a second that she almost reached out to him. She gazed at him, utterly overwhelmed by how he had made her feel. Never, not even in the first flush of their relationship when she had thought Keith was the be-all and end-all, had he been able to inspire such a physical reaction. Which was scary. Very scary. But exhilarating and thrilling too. She hadn't known it was possible to feel so wholly alive.

'I want you, Beth,' he said with remarkable coolness considering she felt she was about to spontaneously combust, 'but as I said, I'm in no hurry. I've never yet taken a woman who wasn't totally and completely ready, mind and body. I'm not about to start with you. That's a promise, OK?'

She nodded helplessly. Speech was beyond her.

'So we have the odd date, see each other when I'm up in these parts, nothing heavy. You learn about me and I learn about you. We might like what we find out, we might not.' The piercing eyes with their black lashes looked down for a moment and when his lids rose again, his gaze fixed on her face. 'But it'll be a good summer,' he said lazily. 'A very good summer indeed.'

CHAPTER SIX

CATHERINE WAS DEFINITELY bright-eyed and bushy-tailed when they walked into the hotel bar some minutes later, her gaze moving searchingly over her sister. Beth tried to ignore the silent question in Catherine's eyes and join the small talk Travis was engaging in but it was hard. For one thing, her brain was still trying to assess just what had happened in the car, and another was the fact that Travis had taken her hand as they'd walked into the hotel and seemed in no hurry to let go.

She stuttered and stumbled her way through the conversation—a conversation which Travis kept flowing with effortless ease having metamorphosed into the perfect charming dinner companion—but it was a huge relief when a waiter appeared at Michael's elbow and informed them their table was ready in the restaurant.

After choosing from the extensive menu it only took Catherine thirty seconds to day, 'I'm just popping to the cloakroom. You coming, Beth?'

The third degree. Beth stared at her sister. But if she didn't go with Catherine now and satisfy her blatant curiosity, her sister would only corner her at some other point during the evening. Better to get it over with.

Once in the ladies' cloakroom, Catherine made no bones about her inquisitiveness but then prevarication had never been one of her sister's attributes.

'So?' Catherine was all agog. 'What gives?'

'What do you mean, what gives?' Beth hedged.

'You were holding hands,' Catherine said gleefully. 'And that looked to be one serious conversation you were having in the car. Don't tell me you were discussing the weather.'

She loved her sister, she really did, but right at this moment she wished Catherine was anywhere but here. How could she explain what she didn't understand herself? Somehow she'd agreed to start dating Travis in the last hour and she would have sworn on oath such a thing was ludicrous this morning. Beth took a deep breath. 'We're friends,' she stated. Then, when her sister gave a horsey snort, she added, 'Just friends. I mean it, Catherine. We've agreed we might see each other now and again when Travis is up here but on a very casual basis. No strings attached, just nice and easy.'

'But you *have* agreed to see him?' Catherine beamed.

'I just said, didn't I?' Beth tried to keep the irritation out of her voice but her sister's smiling face had a definite 'I told you so' edge to it. 'But it's absolutely no strings attached,' she repeated in case Catherine had missed it first time.

'I've seen the way he looks at you.' Catherine was almost purring. 'He's hooked.'

'*Catherine.*' Beth frowned warningly. 'It's not like that. Look, he's already told me he's been in love with someone who didn't feel the same and he'll never get over her.'

'He said that?' Catherine's face dropped. 'Really?'

Well, he had practically. Beth nodded. 'So it's no use getting your hopes up on his side and you know how I feel about the prospect of commitment. Never again.'

'Never's a long time.' Catherine nodded wisely.

'Not in this case,' Beth said firmly. 'Believe me.'

'And if anyone could change your mind, my money's on Travis.'

'You'd lose your money, Cath. Every last penny. I don't mind the odd date but that's all this can ever be.'

They stared at each other for a moment and then Catherine sighed disappointedly. 'OK, I'll take your word for it—for now.'

'Thanks,' said Beth wryly. 'Good of you.'

'But, for what it's worth, I think he's a perfect gem.'

'I don't think Travis is a perfect anything.'

'You know what I mean.' Catherine wrinkled her small nose. 'He's gorgeous, Beth. And I can tell you fancy him,' she added slyly. 'You do, don't you?' she added when Beth didn't say anything. 'It's as plain as the nose on your face.'

Beth hauled her lip gloss out of her bag and pretended to concentrate on renewing her make-up before she said, 'Course I do, who wouldn't? But I'm not the sort of woman who could pop into his bed now and again for a quick spot of sex, no questions asked.'

If she'd hoped to shock her sister into leaving well alone, she failed. Catherine said soberly, 'Then perhaps you ought to try and change.'

Catherine! Now it was Beth who was shocked. 'You've never advocated that sort of carry on,' she said accusingly.

'And I still wouldn't in the usual run of things.' Catherine stared at her. 'But this isn't the norm. Your life hasn't been normal for months and months. Keith was an absolute swine and I don't pretend to know how you must have felt through all that, especially with Mum and Dad going, but I think it's high time you had a bit of fun. You're thirty, Beth, not eighty odd. You've got every chance of meeting someone really nice in the future and perhaps settling down and having a family, but for now just let your hair down. Go mad, step out of character. Be—'

'Irresponsible and harebrained?' Beth put in drily.

'I was going to say flirty.' Catherine grinned at her. 'But irresponsible and harebrained wouldn't do you any harm either. And I've got the idea Travis would be a fantastic initiation into that way of life. He'd be an animal between the sheets,' she finished a little dreamily.

Beth could hardly believe this was Catherine speaking. In spite of all her extrovert ways and bubbly personality, her sister had always been somewhat on the prim side morally.

Her face must have revealed what she was thinking because in the next moment Catherine hugged her, laughter in her voice when she said, 'Go for it, girl. That's my advice. Have a summer to remember.'

'Travis said something similar.'

'Did he? There you are, then. He's a man after my own heart.'

Beth eyed her sister sternly. 'Catherine,

Michael is a man after your own heart and he is nothing like Travis.'

'Ah, but variety is the spice of life.' And then Catherine's voice lost its laughter and she took Beth's face between her hands, her eyes soft as she said, 'Don't let Keith ruin another day, another hour, another *moment,* Neddy. He's not worth it— he never was.'

'I know.' Beth was touched by the love shining out of her sister's face but how could she explain that something had been lost when she'd found out the man she had married was a stranger? Catherine and Michael were so happy and she was glad about that, more than glad, but as her sister had said herself, she couldn't know how she felt. She was thankful Catherine would never have to. The ability to trust a member of the opposite sex had been torn out of her that night as she had listened to Anna speak and she knew she had changed radically from that point on.

As Catherine disappeared into one of the cloak-room's cubicles Beth stared at herself in the mirror. Pensive eyes looked back at her and suddenly she felt impatient with herself.

OK, so perhaps she couldn't trust a man again and certainly the possibility of ever settling down and having a family as Catherine had suggested was a non-starter, but that didn't mean she had to spend the rest of her life without male company. She had all the rest of her life ahead of her and she could make of it what she would. Travis had said he was happy to take things at her pace so she had nothing to lose. Nothing at all. It would be foolish not to at least have a stab at this.

She nodded to the reflection, feeling happier, and as Catherine joined her again she said lightly, 'OK, big sis, I'll take your advice for once. I'll date Travis for a while as long as we both want to and see where it goes, and I won't rule anything out in the bed stakes. How's that?'

'Good.' Nudging her out of the way, Catherine peered into the mirror and then straightened. 'Very good,' she added as she turned to look at Beth. 'In fact, extremely good, I'd say.' And with that she took Beth's arm and they left the cloakroom.

Although Travis—and Michael too, if it came to it—knew nothing of their conversation in the ladies' cloakroom, Beth felt as shy as if the men had been listening as she and Catherine sat down at the table. Within moments, though, Travis was making them all laugh, his manner as easy as if he'd known Catherine and Michael for years instead of just an hour or so.

It set the mood for the evening, an evening which turned out to be hugely enjoyable. Probably because of the heart-to-heart with Catherine and more especially the decision she'd made at the end of it, Beth found herself laughing more than she had since the end of her marriage. Since before then, actually, because Keith hadn't had much of a sense of humour. Whereas Travis's was wicked and entertaining if a little on the cynical side at times.

The meal was delicious and they lingered over coffee and liqueurs for ages. Eventually, though, Beth made noises about leaving. It was crazy, really crazy, but her heart had been in her mouth the last little while at the thought of being alone with Travis again. Excitement, sexual anticipation and sheer fear were vying for first place in her breast and she was blowed if she knew which one was winning.

Travis was unlike any other man she had ever met, that was the trouble, she told herself when, having made their goodbyes to a smiling Catherine and Michael, they walked out to his car. It wasn't just that he was inordinately sexy—although he was. Or totally in control of himself and everyone else—although he was. Or even that the whole of him—looks, personality, everything oozed a magnetism that was lethal. It was the other side of him, the tender, caring side which she had glimpsed a few times now that was compellingly attractive. Or perhaps it was a combination of all those things. She didn't know any more but she wanted to see him when he was up in this neck of the woods, even though she knew it was madness.

'Enjoyed yourself?'

His voice was lazy as he opened the car door for her and she slid inside before she said, 'Yes, it was lovely to see Catherine and Michael again,' although she knew that wasn't strictly what he'd been asking.

'And me?' As he joined her in the car shivers of something warm and not at all unpleasant trickled over her nerve-endings. 'Was it lovely to see me again?'

He was laughing at her; the devilish glint in the grey eyes would have told her even if he wasn't smiling. Unfortunately, as she'd watched him get in the car, images of what he would look like naked had blown her thought processes and Beth found she couldn't come back with an appropriate put-down. Instead she said a little shakily, 'We had a nice evening, didn't we?'

'Oh, we did, Beth,' he said solemnly. 'We had a very nice evening, as it happens. The first of many, I hope.'

Beth exhaled. Sitting here in the shadowed car park, his nearness was excruciatingly real. Fantasy meeting reality.

'But there were a couple of things that weren't to my taste.' He eyed her lazily, his voice smoky.

If she didn't want him to kiss her she shouldn't ask what they were, she knew that. The look on the dark rugged face said so. 'What were they?' she said weakly.

'The first was that there were too many damn people about.' He lifted a hand and stroked the side of her flushed face. 'Which created the second, namely that I couldn't give in to the urge to do this.'

The kiss was long and hungry and satisfyingly deep. Beth wondered if he knew just how extraordinarily good he was at kissing and what a turn-on it would be to any woman. Probably so. In fact a sure-fire certainty. And then she stopped thinking and just gave herself up to the mindless pleasure he was creating.

She was ruffled and dishevelled by the time he settled back into his own seat but alive from the top of her head to the tips of her toes with sheer pulsating sensation.

'You taste of brandy and chocolate mint,' he said throatily as he started the car without looking at her again.

Which was just as well. She needed every second she could get to compose herself. She was relieved her voice sounded fairly normal and not at all like she was feeling inside when she retorted, 'It was you who insisted I have the brandy, remember? I was quite happy to stick with just coffee.'

'Oh, I'm not complaining.' The powerful car nosed out of the car park on to the road with the grace of a big cat. 'In fact, remind me always to take my brandy that way.'

She smiled. 'OK.' She could do this. She could flirt too.

He gave her a slow grin in return before looking back at the road ahead.

They continued on in silence and with every mile Beth was questioning herself. Travis's kisses made her realise that there was more, much more to sex than she had ever realised before because certainly Keith hadn't made her feel a tenth of what Travis did. A hundredth. His sexual expertise was captivating and so was his charm, and it was that which she found frightening about him. Because it made her feel…vulnerable. And she had promised herself she would never be vulnerable again.

But she wasn't, not really, she told herself quickly. Not in a way where she could be badly hurt again anyway. This was just a thing of the flesh and as such not to be compared with the devastation she'd suffered when her marriage had ended so horribly. She had to keep things in perspective here.

Things? Or Travis? As the thought hit she slanted a glance at him under her eyelashes.

Because keeping Travis in perspective might be harder than it sounded.

The sky was velvet-black and pierced with stars as they drove on through the Shropshire countryside, but although Travis was quiet and so was she Beth felt the atmosphere within the car was electric. Did he sense it? She couldn't tell. He was his normal relaxed self outwardly, steering the powerful car with little effort.

Eventually they turned off into the lane which led down to her cottage and then Travis's house, and now Beth found her heart was racing. Would he suggest seeing her tomorrow? Would he expect to come in now? He'd spoken of taking things slow and easy but what did that mean to a man like him?

Alarm began to overwhelm her. She'd insinuated to Catherine that she might consider sleeping with Travis in the future. How could she think such a thing? How could she contemplate going to bed with a man who didn't love her but only felt physical desire? But then had Keith loved her? She'd thought he did but she'd been proved wrong. Perhaps Travis's way was the more honest, at least.

When Travis brought the car to a stop outside her gate Beth knew she wasn't nearly ready for an affair. If he wanted to come in she was going to have to make it very plain a goodnight kiss was all he could expect, she told herself frantically.

He didn't. He merely left the car and walked round the bonnet to open her door, helping her out and then pushing open her gate. 'I'll watch you in,' he said coolly, before pulling her into him and kissing her so thoroughly she was vitally aware of the muscled strength of his body and how aroused he was. Nevertheless it was he who ended the kiss, firmly putting her from him and sending her on her way to the front door on trembling legs.

Harvey bound out as soon as she opened the door and after a cursory welcome made straight for Travis, refusing to return to the house until Travis walked him back.

'He's not normally like this,' Beth said apologetically. 'It's just that he's taken to you.'

A small smile lifted the corners of Travis's mouth. A dry, self-deprecating smile. 'If it helps my case with his mistress I've no objection,' he said softly. He came closer and lifted her chin. 'And I do need all the help I can get, don't I, Beth?'

He had known she was panicking as they had drawn up outside the cottage. She stared at him and then made a small helpless gesture with her hands. 'It isn't you, not as such,' she stammered. 'I'm just not ready…' She shook her head. 'Travis, I'm confused about so many things still.'

'I know,' he said even more softly. 'Or you would be in my bed right now. Goodnight, Beth.'

This time the kiss merely brushed her lips and in the next moment he turned and walked away, sliding into the car and disappearing into the night without a backward glance.

Beth stood for some long minutes staring after him while Harvey nosed about the garden. It was very still and quiet, the warm air scented with the tang of the trees surrounding the cottage and just the faintest echo of woodsmoke.

He hadn't mentioned seeing her again. Her heart began to thump. Had she put him off with her nerves and jitters? Perhaps on reflection he wasn't too keen on getting involved, however lightly, with someone who was carrying a whole load of baggage. Travis would be able to have his pick of many women; he didn't need to waste time with her.

Harvey returned to her side, pushing his cold wet nose in her hand. She gazed down at the big dog and then crouched down and took the furry face in her hands, ruffling his fur as she said, 'What am I doing, Harvey? Have I gone mad or what? Has all this solitude turned my brain?'

Her answer was a long pink tongue across her nose and, laughing now, she stood up. She was thinking too much. It had become a habit since her marriage had ended. She had to do what Catherine had advised and live each day as it came. If

Travis wanted to see her now and again when he was in these parts that was fine. It didn't prevent him having girlfriends at home in Bristol—he was still a free agent. This was just a casual thing, friendly, that was all. Anything else was up to her; he'd made that plain.

Nodding to the night sky, she clicked her fingers at Harvey and turned and walked into the cottage, refusing to dwell on the fact that her lips were still tingling from that last fleeting kiss. Or what it would mean to be bedded by a man like Travis. She rather suspected she was going to have to do a lot of non-thinking in the coming weeks. But she could handle this if she kept her cool. That was the key.

She shut the door behind her, staring round the room she had left just hours before and wondering why everything seemed different. Then she realised what it was. She was happy.

CHAPTER SEVEN

BETH WAS AWOKEN from a deep dreamless sleep the next morning by someone banging on the front door. She sat up in bed just as Harvey began a frenzied barking and at the same time her alarm clock began caterwauling.

Not the most peaceful start to a Sunday morning, then.

Turning off the alarm, she reached for her big fluffy robe and pulled it on over her skimpy nightdress, knotting the belt firmly as she walked to the front door, shushing Harvey in the process. Still dazed with sleep, she didn't even stop to brush her hair.

'Hi.' Travis was on the doorstep and he grinned at her, holding out some bags. 'Breakfast. It's a beautiful day and I thought we shouldn't waste a minute of it as I have to leave tonight.'

Beth felt like a dormouse rudely awoken from hibernation. Trying to pull herself together, she said, 'What time is it?'

'Nine o'clock,' he said as though *everyone* was up by then.

She brushed back a lock of hair from her face. 'I haven't even showered.' Whereas he looked as fresh as a daisy.

'No?' He considered her with warm eyes. 'You look great to me. I like my women tousled and sexy.'

She probably looked as sexy as if she'd been pulled through a hedge backwards. Beth stood aside. 'Come in,' she said reluctantly. 'I'll put the coffee pot on.'

'No need.' He followed her into the cottage and then took her into his arms before she could protest, kissing her in such a way she woke up— fast. It was a nice way to wake up.

Then she was free again and he went through to the kitchen, calling over his shoulder, 'The croissants are warm and I've brought homemade gooseberry preserve and blueberry jam from a shop in the village, so hurry up. I'll put the coffee on.'

Once in the bathroom, Beth showered in sixty seconds flat. She'd taken her bra and pants and a thin sleeveless dress in with her and, after dressing, she quickly brushed her hair and looped it into a high ponytail on top of her head. It'd have to do. If he wanted a fully coiffured, perfectly made-up female he shouldn't arrive unannounced.

When she walked through to the kitchen it was

clear from the look on Travis's face that he didn't want any of those things. He smiled at her, a slow sexy smile, before saying, 'You're beautiful, you know that, don't you? Even with mud all over your face that first time I saw you, I knew you were beautiful.'

'I don't think that was mud, Travis,' she said drily.

He grinned. 'I was being polite.'

'Right.' She was determined to keep things light and uncomplicated. Survival technique. She glanced at the tiny breakfast bar, which was covered with plates of exotic-looking cold meat, several cheeses, cold salmon, fresh fruit, different types of rolls— still warm, if the smell was anything to go by—little boxes of cereal and a jar of honey, as well as the croissants he had mentioned. Her eyes widened. 'You brought all this?' It was a veritable feast.

'Courtesy of the wonderful delicatessen in the village. The honey is from their own bees, by the way, and it's the best I've ever tasted.' He indicated two trays he had set, complete with glasses of orange juice. 'I thought we'd eat alfresco. Come and fill your plate and we'll take it into the garden.'

Beth found herself rebelling against the way he had taken over. Nodding her head at the coffee pot, she said, 'I'll just have a coffee for now, thanks. Give my stomach a chance to wake up properly,' she added pointedly.

'Fine. I'll see to it.'

He was so unconcerned that Beth immediately felt churlish. She glanced at Harvey, who was sitting ramrod straight, his whole being focused on a bag on the draining board. 'What's the matter with him?' she asked in surprise.

'He knows there's a knuckle bone in there.' Travis smiled his slightly lopsided smile. 'I'm not above bribery and corruption.'

'You don't need to try with Harvey,' Beth said flatly. 'I think he already prefers you to me.' She wasn't joking.

'I wasn't talking about Harvey.' Travis had been pouring two mugs of coffee as they'd spoken and now he gave Beth hers, adding, 'Go out into the garden and I'll bring the bone for Harvey to eat while we drink our coffee.'

With an ecstatic Harvey gnawing on a huge bone, which had enough meat left on it to feed a family of four, Beth tried to concentrate on anything other than the closeness of the big male body sitting next to her in the warm sunshine a minute later. The little wooden bench was just right for one but definitely on the cosy side for two. Travis's thigh was pressed against hers and she could feel the warmth of his muscled flesh through the thin material of her dress, his arm outstretched at the back of her along the wooden seat bringing her into the circle of his body even though he wasn't overtly touching her.

The coffee was scalding hot but she sipped at it nevertheless, trying to dispel the vibrations pulsating from the core of her. Pointless to tell herself she could control the effect this powerful sexual chemistry between them had on her. When he was near like this reason went out of the window. Using Harvey as an excuse, she bent down and stroked the dog's rough fur, earning herself a quick doggy grin and lick of her hand before he went back to the business in hand.

'Good natured animal, isn't he?' Travis said above her. 'Some animals growl if they're touched when they've got a prize. Worried it's going to be taken away, I guess.'

'I could take anything away from Harvey,' Beth said quietly. 'He trusts me.'

'How long have you had him?'

She couldn't do this. She couldn't sit and talk with the feel and delicious smell of him making her legs weak and her pulse race. She had put some cake out on the small bird table in a corner of the tiny garden the night before; now she used the fact some crumbs had fallen on to the floor as an excuse to move from the bench. After picking up the fragments of cake, she scattered them on the bird table and then seated herself on the tub of flowers she had sat on when they had been in the garden together once before. It was only then she said, 'Harvey was a gift from my sister when I moved into my flat over a year and a half ago. He was just a little puppy then.'

Travis glanced at the powerful jaws which were making short work of the bone. 'Not so little now. Do you take him with you when you work?'

Beth nodded. 'Any time I can't, Catherine has him. My little nephew, James, loves him and Harvey's as gentle as a lamb with him. I'd never had a dog before and it would never have occurred to me to get one but I don't know what I'd do without him now. Harvey's more than a dog, he's…' She stopped, wondering if he would think she was silly.

'A friend?' Travis said softly.

Beth nodded again. 'My best friend,' she said a little defiantly. 'He helped me through the worst time of my life and I'll forever be grateful to him.' Immediately she regretted saying it. It wasn't the way to keep things light and casual. But it was too late now.

'Unconditional love.' He finished his coffee in one gulp. 'Animals have it in abundance but it's a rare quality in *Homo sapiens*.' He leant forward slightly and every nerve in her body responded. 'It must have been tough,' he said quietly, 'and I'm sorry you had to endure something so terrible through no fault of your own. Life sucks sometimes.'

She looked back at him, an echo of the old anguish streaking through her briefly. 'When I look back it was losing my parents the way I did that hurts most.' Her voice was so low he had to lean further forward to hear her. 'They were wonderful people, the best parents in the world. Funny, but my dad never did get on with Keith. My mum thought he was lovely; Keith had a way with women—' her voice held a note of bitterness for a moment '—but my dad was always very wary of him. He wanted us to wait for a while before we got married but...' She shrugged. 'Love's blind.'

'Beth, anyone can be fooled by someone who is determined and cunning enough. It was no reflection on your judgement or anything else. Bad things happen to good people.'

She stared at him and her eyes were huge and shadowed; she was bewildered at how much she had opened up to him when she had been determined not to. 'Some people are more gullible than others.' The little catch in her voice told him this was something very important. 'I didn't think I was like that but I must be. How else could I have married someone, lived with him, *loved* him, and not have a clue what he was really like? I wouldn't have believed it was possible if it hadn't happened to me.'

'It's possible.' He reached out and touched her mouth tenderly with his finger, his voice deep and smoky. 'But, as I said, it's nothing to do with being gullible in your case. Keith was something that crawled out from under a stone, without morals and principles, and that gave him power of a kind. You were unfortunate enough to have your life touched by him but you had the strength and courage to do something about it. He won't prosper, Beth. Not in the long run. His kids won't respect him—they might not even love him or want anything to do with him when they're older—and eventually any woman he gets involved with will see him for what he is. He'll die a lonely bitter old man one day.'

'You don't know that.' She shook her head, her voice shaking. 'And how do you know I'm not gullible? Why is my case different from lots of others where women are taken for a ride time and time again?'

'I know you.' His voice was firm and warm.

'But you don't. We only met a few weeks ago. You know hardly anything about me. I might be a serial victim.'

Travis gave her a crooked smile. 'I know you,' he repeated softly. 'And it's nothing to do with time. It happens like that sometimes. You're no more a victim than I am.'

She was very pale, her haunted eyes warning him that he had taken her to the limit of her endurance for the moment. He stood up, his voice matter-of-fact as though they had just been discussing the weather, when he said, 'I'm for breakfast, how about you? Coming to choose for yourself?'

'You…you go and help yourself. I'll come in a minute when I've finished my coffee.'

When he disappeared into the house Beth went limp and she knew she was trembling. She hoped Travis hadn't noticed. How had he made her say all that? And what had he meant by that last comment—that he knew her? She pressed her hand to her heart as it pounded against her chest. She didn't want any man to know her, to get too close. This idea of them seeing each other was a bad one—she had to tell him she had changed her mind. She hadn't come here to get involved with anyone, least of all a member of the male sex, and *especially* one as—her mind sought for a word to describe Travis and failed, she compromised on—unusual as Travis.

She stood up, resolved to get it over and done with immediately. Her stomach churning, she walked into the kitchen and then stopped, surprised, when it was empty. A moment later Travis appeared, his manner casual and his voice easy when he said, 'Left the newspapers in the car.' He reached for his tray as he spoke, his plate piled high with enough food for a rugby team. 'I'll see you outside; don't be long.'

He'd disappeared before she could say anything, and when she joined him outside a minute or two later he was sitting on the tub she'd vacated, a newspaper spread out on the floor in front of him in which he was apparently engrossed as he ate. Beth sat down on the bench, feeling at a loss. She didn't know how to start now. Somehow the atmosphere had changed again. 'You don't look very comfortable perched on there,' she began.

'I'm fine.' He didn't raise his head from the newspaper and his voice was preoccupied.

Beth gave up and selected a newspaper from the pile he'd placed at one end of the bench, biting into a croissant as she began to read. She'd say something later; there was plenty of time.

It was a warm, lazy Sunday morning. When they had eaten their fill—Travis packing away an inordinate amount of food—Beth made some more coffee and they continued to read the papers in the sunshine, sitting side by side on the bench now. Fat bumble bees buzzed among the tubs of flowers, a family of bright-eyed sparrows chattered and squabbled as they cleared the cake from the bird table and Harvey, replete and satisfied, dozed and dreamed doggy dreams at their feet.

It was a perfect summer's idyll—or it would have been if Beth hadn't been so edgy. But, like the night before at the hotel, Travis had moved into charming companion mode. After stretching out his long legs and tilting his head back against the back of the bench, he appeared to doze for a while, before suddenly standing up and hauling her to her feet.

'Walk,' he announced. 'Burn off some calories for lunch.'

Harvey had heard the magic word and so she couldn't object.

With Harvey gambolling on in front, they walked through the woods, breathing in the delicious smell of good damp earth underfoot, before walking the banks of a sparkling tranquil river. Or it had been tranquil before Harvey arrived. It was at moments like these, as the big dog splashed and charged about in an ecstasy of enjoyment, that Beth realised he was still just a puppy in spite of his size.

Travis made her laugh often as they walked and she gradually found herself relaxing and just enjoying the beautiful morning. Daisies, buttercups, rich white clover and many other wild flowers Beth didn't know the names of dotted the grass at their feet, the perfume of pine heavy in the warm air.

Travis had taken her hand at the beginning of the walk and she hadn't objected, wondering if he would pause and kiss her at some point. He didn't. He kept the conversation light and amusing and unthreatening, whether by design or accident Beth wasn't sure. She only knew that her emotions had shifted yet again and now the thought of finishing with him was off the agenda. Which made her the most fickle of females, she admitted soberly, as they began to retrace their steps to the cottage. But she just didn't seem to know her own mind where Travis was concerned.

'What?' Too late Beth realised she must have been staring at him and the piercing grey gaze was now trained on her face. 'What's the matter?'

'Nothing.' She forced a smile. 'Nothing's the matter.'

He stopped, enclosing her within his arms, but loosely. 'Don't buy it,' he said evenly. 'What were you thinking?'

She thought swiftly. 'I was just wondering about that.' She touched the scar on his face. 'How you got it.'

He looked at her and she knew he didn't believe her but he didn't pursue the matter, taking her hand again and lacing her fingers through his as they began to walk on. 'I had a brother,' he said unemotionally, 'Kirk. He was two years older than me. Shortly after my mother met my stepfather he took Kirk and I fishing for the day. The boat overturned in the river when my stepfather overbalanced; he'd been messing about, showing off. Kirk got entangled in some weeds and stuff, couldn't surface. I shouted to my stepfather to help me but he was more bothered about saving his own skin. By the time I got Kirk to the surface I'd had to come up for air umpteen times. He didn't have a chance.' He touched the scar on his face. 'There were all manner of things in the river; I don't know what I caught my face on. I didn't even feel it at the time. It wasn't until we got to the hospital it started hurting.'

'Oh, Travis.' Beth was appalled. She stopped, causing him to halt too and look at her. 'I'm so sorry,' she said weakly. 'That's terrible.'

He nodded. 'Yes, it was.' For a moment something worked in his face and then he got control again. 'My stepfather insisted he didn't help because he couldn't swim and had only just managed to get to the bank by a fluke. I didn't believe him. I'd seen him in the water and he could swim all right. But my mother chose to accept his story.' He smiled grimly. 'You talked about blind love earlier and that really was blind love. You had no choice in your situation, no warning. She did. All the danger signals were there with bells on.'

Beth stared at him. 'Did Sandra believe you?'

'Not at the time but later she did, when she was living with them after they'd married. He's an…unpleasant man.'

'But your mother's still with him?' she asked softly.

'She won't leave.' He shrugged. 'Misguided loyalty.'

It bothered him greatly, she could tell. Suddenly she had the crazy impulse to wrap her arms round him and kiss him, an overwhelming flood of tenderness consuming her. It was enough to shock her into taking a sharp emotional step backwards. 'I'm sorry,' she said again, beginning to walk once more.

He shrugged. 'It was a long time ago now.'

She had been referring to the fact that his mother was still with a man who apparently was no good, but she didn't elaborate further in view of her traitorous hormones. Fortunately—or perhaps *un*fortunately, Beth wasn't sure—Harvey provided a distraction at that moment by catapulting up covered in wet mud and holding something which had obviously been dead a long time in his jaws. In the resulting mayhem—Beth had to admit afterwards she'd behaved in a very girly way by screaming and trying to avoid the smell of what he was carrying—their previous conversation was lost, and once back at the cottage things returned to light mode again.

Travis very kindly offered to bath Harvey before they left him to go and lunch at a little country pub he knew, and Beth let him. The smell emanating from the big dog was even more disgusting than the putrid gunge she'd slipped in her first night at the cottage—which was saying something. She wondered if it was such a good idea, though, when Travis stripped off his shirt before leading a crest-fallen Harvey to the shower. And she knew it *definitely* hadn't been a good idea when the two of them returned, Harvey sweet-smelling and Travis looking so sexy her mouth dried instantly.

He'd got wet, as his black jeans testified, but it was his thickly muscled torso gleaming like oiled silk which really caused her blood to heat. The black curly hair on his chest was glistening with tiny droplets of water and beneath the black denim his thighs looked hard and powerful. It was an un-compromisingly male body. Virile. Strong. Beth just looked—she couldn't help it.

'He's feeling a little sorry for himself.' Travis indicated Harvey with a wave of his hand and it was only then she managed to pull herself together and act naturally, fussing Harvey while Travis pulled on his shirt. She could still see the broad tanned shoulders in her mind's eye, and the way the hair on his chest narrowed to a thin line down into his jeans. He would be incredible naked. A rugged Adonis with a charisma that was so much more powerful than mere handsomeness.

'I'll just get my handbag,' she murmured, scampering into her bedroom and then leaning against the shut door for a moment or two to compose herself. She lifted her hands to her hot cheeks. Thank goodness he couldn't read her mind. He'd think she was the original sex-starved female. Well, maybe she was at that. She smiled wryly, her sense of humour coming to the rescue. Now she had found the on button of her libido she just didn't seem able to turn it off.

Travis was his normal cool urbane self when she joined him. Harvey, on the other hand, was definitely out of sorts and sulking. She smiled at Travis and then bent and hugged Harvey—she'd much rather it was the other way round if she was truthful—before saying, 'Do you want to change your jeans before we go for lunch?'

Travis shook his head. 'I'll soon dry in the sun,' he said lazily. 'The place where we're eating has a garden leading down to the river and I've reserved a table outside.'

Beth hoped she didn't look as flustered as she felt as they left the cottage and walked to Travis's car. Ridiculous, but she almost felt she'd seen him naked. But then she'd seen a naked man before, for goodness' sake, hundreds of times. Keith hadn't been diffident about showing off his body. So why should Travis partly clothed affect her a hundred times more than Keith had ever done totally in the buff?

She was still pondering her capriciousness when they arrived at the charming olde-worlde pub twenty minutes later. The centuries old building, complete with thatched roof and brasses and an enormous old fireplace with ancient range, was packed to the hilt when they walked in, but almost immediately a small plump peroxide-blonde woman was at their side, her face beaming. 'Travis!' She flung her arms round him and gave him a smacker of a kiss full on the lips. 'About time you showed your face here. I was only saying to Dave the other day we hadn't seen you for weeks.'

'Sorry, Mavis.' Travis disentangled himself from the embrace and drew Beth forward. 'Meet Beth,' he said softly. 'Beth, this is Mavis, the landlady of the establishment, who is also married to my oldest friend, Dave. It was when I was visiting them some years ago I heard about the house for sale and decided to buy a weekend place here.'

'Pleased to meet you, Beth.'

As Mavis turned to her, Beth became aware she was being scrutinised very thoroughly by a pair of blue eyes surrounded by panda make-up. A little taken aback, she murmured, 'Hello, Mavis. I'm pleased to meet you too.'

'I've kept your table once Dave said you were coming.' Mavis turned back to Travis, adding, 'Your jeans are wet. What on earth have you been doing?'

'Washing Beth's dog. We took him for a walk after breakfast and he managed to disgrace himself.'

'Right.' Mavis nodded. 'Bad as your two then, is he?'

Beth didn't know if Travis was aware that Mavis had put two and two together and made ten with that statement about after breakfast, but she'd seen the gleam in the other woman's eye as she'd glanced at them both. Quickly now she said, 'Travis arrived on my doorstep this morning having bought up most of the goodies in the local delicatessen, so if I don't do full justice to your lunch it's his fault.'

'Oh, don't you worry, dear, we've all sorts to choose from. If you want something light the salmon in prawn and dill sauce is lovely. You two go through to the garden and I'll bring your drinks to you. What are you having?'

Having given Mavis their order and waved at

Dave, who was manning the bar with the help of a couple of barmaids, Travis took her hand and led her through the pub and out into the garden. It wasn't at all what Beth had expected, having an almost cottagey feel to it rather than the smooth lawns covered with umpteen picnic tables such establishments usually boasted. Small wrought iron tables and chairs were dotted here and there between riotous flowerbeds and sweet-smelling bushes and tubs, several trees providing welcome shade from the hot sun in some places. The whole garden was on a very slight slope which led down to the banks of the river, a small fence providing protection for children from the deep water, and an army of ducks and swans scattered along the bank on the other side.

Travis stopped at a small table for two set slightly apart from the others under the shade of a silver birch tree which overlooked the glittering water, pulling out her chair and then, once she was seated, sitting down himself. It was only then he said, and very quietly, 'Why so defensive, Beth? Is it really so unthinkable for anyone to imagine we might be lovers?'

She stared at him, flushing. 'I don't know what you mean,' she lied. 'No one's said anything about us being lovers.'

'I saw your face.' The grey gaze was unblinking.

'Travis—'

'What it is about me that makes the thought of our being intimate so repugnant?'

He was angry. He was hiding it under the smooth controlled exterior and his voice was without heat, but she knew he was angry. Swallowing hard, she murmured, 'It's not like that. I've told you I can't get involved with anyone; I didn't want Mavis to get the idea we were serious, that's all.'

'It's not can't, Beth. It's won't.'

'What?' She broke their shared gaze, her cheeks burning.

'You said you can't get involved with anyone. That's not true. You're a free agent. You can please yourself exactly what you do with the rest of your life.' He leant back in his chair, surveying her from chilled grey eyes. 'I told you I have no expectations and that we can take this as slowly as you want, so could you do me the favour of at least pretending to relax and enjoy our being together. It's getting a mite uncomfortable, this feeling that you expect me to jump on you at any moment and have my wicked way.'

'I don't.' There was a lump expanding like dough in her throat. Everything had suddenly gone wrong and she was shaken by the swiftness of it. And it certainly wasn't the fact that she expected him to force the issue sexually that was at the heart of her edginess—more that she might not be able to keep her hands off him for much longer. But she could hardly admit that. She had to say something, though, and she didn't know what.

'No?' He leant forward and took her hand. 'Then why are you trembling right now?' he asked evenly. 'You make me feel like the Marquis de Sade, damn it.'

Self-protection vied with confusion and guilt. She didn't want to make Travis feel bad but she didn't know how to explain where she was at without opening herself up to being vulnerable. And that would give him even more power over her than he had at present. She fought with herself for a few endless moments and then took a deep breath. 'I'm frightened I might grow to like you more than I want to,' she said at last. 'I wasn't ready to meet anyone when I met you. I didn't want to be attracted to a man for a long, long time.'

His eyes continued to hold her for another moment as he searched her face. 'That's all it is?'

All it is? Cheek. She had just bared her soul and he acted as though it was nothing. She nodded.

He sighed softly but something in his face had mellowed and he looked like the Travis she was used to again. 'Beth, I've never been in any doubt that you need to sort yourself out,' he said drily.

'And frankly I prefer my bed partners to be there because they are one hundred per cent certain they want to be. OK? It's not just your body I want between my sheets—' she shivered, she couldn't help it, and the keen grey gaze deepened '—but you. Understand? Mind, soul and spirit. I'm greedy,' he added unrepentantly.

The sky was very blue at the back of him and somewhere down on the river bank she could hear ducks quack-quacking, the light summer breeze stroking her face with its warmth. She wondered what his reaction would be if she asked him to take her straight home to his bed because every fibre of her being wanted it. It would cut through everything she had said in the last minutes but nevertheless the words hovered on her tongue.

'Here we are, then. Sorry about the delay, but it's madness in there.' Mavis bustled up with the bottle of wine Travis had ordered, two glasses and a couple of menus. 'Dave will see you later,' she added to Travis, 'and he said to say he's told chef to put a pair of lamb shanks by in case you fancy your usual. He braises them in a port and redcurrant sauce.' She turned to Beth, including her in the conversation. 'And frankly we can never get enough to satisfy demand. But of course there's plenty of other dishes to choose from if you're not overly hungry. I'll leave you to it, then.' She flashed them both a beaming smile. 'I'll be back in five minutes to take your order.' And with that she sailed off.

'She's a bundle of energy.' Travis had noticed Beth's slightly bemused expression. 'Whereas Dave's the most laid-back soul in the world. A definite case of opposites attracting, but their marriage is rock solid.'

'How long have they been married?' said Beth, glad to move to a safe topic and secretly aghast at how near she had come to renouncing all her hitherto sensible demands that they take things slowly. Thank goodness Mavis had come when she did.

'Ten years. We were all at university together, although I'd known Dave at school. He proved himself to be a good friend when Kirk died,' Travis said calmly.

Beth stared at him. He had started to pour the wine and his hand was steady, his voice even, but she knew the thought of his brother was painful. She didn't know how she knew but she just did. He was by no means fully over what had happened, but then in such cases perhaps one never really recovered? Maybe the best to hope for was to learn to live with the pain?

She felt too emotional herself to go down that

avenue so instead she said, 'Do they have any children?'

'Five.' And then he smiled the smile that made such a difference to the hard rugged face when her mouth dropped open. 'But there are two sets of twins in there; they run in the family on Mavis's side, apparently. They had a boy first and then two sets of girls. It's bedlam sometimes, according to Dave.'

'Wow.' Beth was genuinely impressed. 'I think I'd have chickened out at three.'

'But you have to take passion into account,' Travis said gravely. 'I gather the last pregnancy was a result of one of those wild nights when they couldn't get enough of each other and precautions were the last thing on their minds.'

Beth refused to blush because she knew that was exactly what he'd had in mind. She also refused to dwell on the smoky quality to his voice and the way he was looking at her. 'Lucky old them.' She reached for her glass of wine and had a good few gulps. There, that was better. The sizzling in her blood was under control again. 'But I should imagine life's a bit hectic with five young children,' she said primly, ignoring the quirk to his mouth. 'Especially with a pub to run.'

'Mavis's parents live with them at the pub; they all went into business together so help's always at hand.' Travis handed her a menu. 'Wouldn't suit me; I'd want my wife all to myself.' His dark eyes stroked over her face and her pulse quickened. 'But they're as happy as bugs in rugs.'

He leant forward again, his fingers tweaking the thin strap of her dress back on to her shoulder from where it had slipped. His touch set her skin on fire and Beth inwardly groaned at her weakness. 'Your skin's like silk,' he murmured. 'Warm silk kissed by the sun, soft and smooth. A man could lose himself in such softness, do you know that?'

She wanted to make some light throwaway comment, something witty which would defuse the moment but without embarrassment, but she couldn't. She just stared at him, her heart thundering in her ears.

'I want to make love to you until you forget what day it is, what month it is, what year, until there is nothing in the world but us and what we're doing to each other. It would be like that, I know it. The rest of the world would fade away as though it didn't exist.' And then he settled himself back in his seat and picked up his menu, his voice suddenly shockingly matter-of-fact as he said, 'But until that day I'll just have to be patient. The lamb's fantastic, by the way. I'd seriously advise you to try it.'

CHAPTER EIGHT

THE LAMB *WAS* FANTASTIC and so was the rest of the meal. They had arrived just as last orders were being taken and by the time they were at the coffee stage the garden was all but deserted and the pub had closed. Mavis and Dave joined them at their table and the four of them sat for a long time talking and laughing, Mavis's parents bringing the children out at one point. The little boy, who looked to be seven or eight, obviously adored Travis and insisted on sitting on his knee for the time that remained, although the girls were taken in for a nap by their grandmother after just a few minutes.

Beth had to admit to herself that she felt all at odds watching Travis with the child. For such a big masculine man he was extraordinarily gentle with the little boy and perfectly relaxed in his role of 'Uncle Travis'. She didn't know why but she hadn't expected him to be so instinctive with children but he was a natural. He'd be one great father.

They left at five o'clock so Mavis and Dave could get ready for opening again at six-thirty, and by then Beth had so many different impressions whirling in her mind that she'd given herself a headache. Every time she was with Travis he seemed to show a different side to himself, or perhaps she should say he showed more of himself, she corrected silently. Whatever, it was disconcerting. She had been hoping the more she got to know him the less she would be attracted to him but the opposite was happening. Which wasn't good. Or was it?

On the ride back to the cottage he said little but Beth was lost in her own thoughts anyway. And they were all about him. Sex with a virtual stranger, just for the hell of it, had never held any appeal for her but the trouble was that Travis was not a stranger any more. Far from it. In fact, she could hardly believe how well she felt she knew him considering they'd only known each other such a short time. And then again, she didn't feel she knew anything about him. Which didn't make sense. Like all of this. The only consistent thing in the whole scenario was her *in*consistency, she thought ruefully. Why on earth Travis was even bothering with her in the first place she didn't know. She must seem like a madwoman to him.

They were back at the cottage. Beth realised

with a little jolt that she hadn't even noticed him draw on to the side of the lane and stop the car. Travis exited the Aston Martin and walked round the bonnet, opening her door and assisting her out of the low-slung car with a hand at her elbow. He walked with her to the front door of the cottage, but as she reached for the key in her handbag his hand closed over hers.

'I'd prefer to say goodnight before Harvey makes an appearance,' he said with good-natured wryness, taking her into his arms before she could say anything.

His mouth closed over hers with a certainty that said any objection wasn't an option, not that Beth wanted to object. In fact she'd been waiting for this moment for the last few hours, she realised helplessly. She gave herself up to the exquisite sensation washing over her, trembling as the kiss deepened and intensified.

Travis had placed a hand in the small of her back to steady her as he moulded her into him, his legs slightly apart as he pleasured himself with the feel of her body and her warm mouth. As she began to kiss him back he made a harsh guttural sound in the base of his throat, his other hand cupping her breast and rubbing the engorged peak with a slow languorous rhythm that sent sharp needles of pleasure into the core of her.

Beth's hands moved to his shoulders, feeling the muscled strength beneath her fingers with a kind of wondering triumph. It was exhilarating to know she could inspire such desire in a man like Travis, and there was no doubt he wanted her. His heart was slamming against the solid wall of his chest and he was breathing hard, his arousal fierce against the soft swell of her belly.

So it came as all the more of a drenching shock when he lifted his mouth from hers a moment later, putting her from him gently but firmly as he said thickly, 'I have to go. I'll see you next week, Beth.'

She stared at him, unable to take in for a second that he was leaving. She didn't want him to go. 'Travis—'

'Goodnight, Beth. Dream of me, OK?'

The control was back, even though he was still breathing hard, his chest rising and falling beneath the thin material of his shirt. But his eyes were focused and steady, his mouth faintly stern as he stepped backwards.

She couldn't say anything more; speech was beyond her as she watched him turn and walk to the Aston Martin crouched in the lane. Everything in her wanted to run after him and beg him to continue what he had begun, but the fact that he had been able to leave her was the thing that stopped her.

She didn't understand him. She didn't understand how he could walk away at a time like this, she thought feverishly as the powerful car disappeared in a cloud of dust. He must have known that she wanted him. He was an experienced man of the world, after all, used to reading sexual signals and unspoken desires. And she hadn't exactly been disguising how she'd felt.

It was Harvey's aggrieved barking that brought her back to reality. As she quickly opened the door the big dog stared at her reproachfully before exiting the house, only to turn and look at her again with a distinctly ill-used expression.

'Yes, OK, he's gone,' Beth said irritably. 'And I'm not too pleased about it either, all right? But it appears he can take or leave us so you'd better get used to it.'

Harvey surveyed her a moment more from soulful brown eyes before marching back into the cottage again, every line of his body stating that as she had incarcerated him inside on a glorious summer afternoon and then deprived him of the company of his favourite human, the least she could do was to set about seeing to his dinner.

By the time she went to bed Beth's equilibrium had begun to stabilise. It would have been a momentous mistake to go to bed with Travis, she assured herself for the umpteenth time as she snuggled under the crisp cotton sheet. The night was too warm for even a summer duvet. Huge mistake. Gigantic. So he'd done her a favour in cutting things short. No question about it. She just wished it had been *her* who had called a halt, that was all. It was galling in the extreme to know she affected him so fleetingly that he could walk away at a time like that.

The owl hooted just outside the bedroom window but the sound didn't thrill her like it usually did.

'I am not going to think about this a moment more.' She said the words out loud, hoping the sound of her voice would clarify things. 'He's gone for another week and that's fine, absolutely fine. If he turns up at the weekend and calls by, no doubt we'll have a nice time. If he doesn't…' There had been life before Travis Black and there would be life after him. All this really wasn't a problem unless she made it one. Simple. So now all she had to do was to go to sleep.

Beth had taken some aspirin for the headache earlier, now she purposefully employed herself in going through the relaxing techniques she had learnt in the aftermath of her marriage break-up. Every time her wayward mind veered Travis's way she brought it back under control. It wasn't easy but she persevered. And persevered. And persevered.

Nevertheless, the sun was already coming up before she drifted off into a troubled sleep populated by disturbing dreams she couldn't remember in the bright clear light of morning. Except that Travis had featured heavily in every one.

The next few days passed by in the lazy pleasant fashion she had got used to since moving to Shropshire. Walks with Harvey, meals when she was hungry, sleep when she was tired. No one to answer to but herself. Except now it wasn't enough. Something was missing. She wasn't brave enough to examine exactly what it was, but as Friday drew near she became as jumpy as a cat on a hot tin roof.

Thursday she spent cleaning the cottage until every surface was shiny and polished and the windows gleamed, and Friday she pottered about in the garden, watering the plants and weeding. The good weather continued in spite of dire warnings on the news that massive storms were expected when the heatwave finally broke.

She heard the car long before she saw it mid-afternoon as she was trying to persuade some tiny pansies to raise their heads in the new flowerbeds she'd created in the front garden. Her heart thudding, she rose to her feet, her hand trembling a little as she shaded her eyes and looked towards the lane outside the cottage garden. Harvey had obviously recognised the sound of the car too because the big dog had galloped over to the garden gate where he now stood, whining excitedly.

By the time Travis exited the Mercedes Estate she had pulled herself together, her voice friendly and her smile warm but not too warm as she called, 'Hi there. You got away earlier this week, then?'

He opened and closed the gate, patting Harvey and then walking up to her before he said, 'Made sure of it,' his voice like dark velvet. 'Nothing would have stopped me leaving.'

'Good.' She didn't know what else to say, not with him so close and looking good enough to eat.

He studied her face for a moment, a half-smile curving his lips. 'Silky soft, tousled and kissable,' he murmured. 'I've been thinking about this all week.' And then he took her into his arms.

His kiss was passionate but even as Beth kissed him back she was aware of his total control over himself. After a while he held her away from him but not before the muscled strength of his body and the scent and feel of him had stirred in her a nervous exhilaration combined with a deep need. 'You've got dirt on your forehead,' he said easily, touching the smudge on her face with a lazy finger. 'How about you go and get cleaned up while I put Harvey with Sheba and Sky in the back of the car and we eat at my place tonight? I've a couple of fillet steaks and some other goodies in the car.'

She nodded, mainly because she didn't trust herself to speak right at that moment. He kissed her again, a fleeting kiss this time, and then let go of her, turning and walking away with Harvey bounding beside him.

Beth was glad of the time to compose herself as she washed and changed out of her vest top and shorts into a soft summer dress. She had missed him the last few days, she admitted to herself as she brushed her hair into a sleek curtain falling either side of her face. She just hadn't realised how much until she had heard his car approaching. But she hadn't missed the message his kiss had been sending. It stated that he intended to play fair in all of this and keep to his promise that they would play the game by her rules, at her pace. Which was good. Or it would have been if she knew what her pace was. As it was, she didn't have a clue.

As she left the house to join Travis and the dogs in the car the first big fat raindrops began to fall and a roll of thunder growled across the sky. But it didn't matter. Nothing mattered because she had the whole weekend with Travis in front of her. Just the thought of it was intoxicating.

She looked at him through the open window of the car and his eyes, as grey as the clouds that had spread across the blue sky, but very clear, smiled back at her. She felt her heart give a little jump as one black eyebrow quirked up and he said, 'Perhaps not the barbecue I was thinking of, after all, but a candlelit dinner instead. How about that?'

'Fine.' She slid into the car, hoping she appeared more cool and self-possessed than she felt. 'Sounds great.'

He leant towards her, his face very close and his heavily lashed eyes glinting as they focused on her mouth. One finger softly touched where his eyes had stroked before moving down the curve of her chin and slowly, very slowly and seductively continuing a path down her throat and into the soft swell of her cleavage. 'Nice dress,' he said throatily before kissing her full on the lips and then starting the car.

'Thank you,' she said primly, her heart racing.

'You're welcome.' He grinned at her, a devilish gleam in his eyes which made her wonder if she should have chosen a dress with a higher neckline.

But this one, a sleeveless shift in pure white with a trim of deep blue, made the most of her recently acquired tan and emphasised the colour of her eyes. And she had wanted to look nice for him. Nice… The word mocked her with its demureness. She didn't want to just look nice for Travis, she wanted—

Beth cut off her thoughts ruthlessly, refusing to acknowledge the noticeable electricity in the air which was nothing to do with the worsening weather and all to do with the big dark man at her side. 'Have you had a good week?' she asked evenly.

'So-so.' He glanced at her. 'Lonely dinners, even more lonely breakfasts.'

Beth swallowed. If he was saying what she thought he was saying... 'You don't have to be lonely on my account,' she said carefully. 'I mean I don't expect you to change your lifestyle because we're seeing each other when you're up in these parts. If you want to...date other women, that's fine.'

'Change my lifestyle?' His voice was steady, expressionless even, but there was the merest something which alerted her to the fact that she had annoyed him. 'What do you think my "lifestyle" consists of, Beth? An orgy of one-night stands? A merry-go-round of bed partners? The little black book by the phone, maybe?'

No, she didn't think that. Travis was not a promiscuous man, she would bet her life on it. He was a highly discriminating and intelligent individual who would want more than mere physical stimulation from any women he was involved with. Quite how she had arrived at this knowledge, Beth wasn't sure, but it was there. 'I didn't mean to insinuate that.' She looked down at her hands, wondering why she was forever destined to mess things up with this man. 'I don't think you are like that at all.'

'No?' He paused significantly. 'Sure about that?'

She raised her head, glancing at the rugged profile. 'Yes, I'm sure,' she said very firmly.

There was a moment of explosive silence. 'Good.' One small word but his voice was warm again. 'But, for the record, let me just emphasise that one woman at a time is more than enough for me, especially if the woman in question happens to be a blue-eyed blonde architect. OK? However things turn out between us. Do you understand what I'm getting at here?'

'I was just trying to say—'

'I know what you were trying to say, Beth,' he said evenly. This time the silence was shorter but just as charged before he continued, 'But I expect fidelity in return; it works both ways. Just so we both know where we stand.'

Did he seriously think there was even a chance of her being interested in another man when he was around? And then she immediately checked herself, altering the thought to—when she had just been through a traumatic divorce? 'I wouldn't dream of seeing anyone else,' she said with very real indignation. 'Of course I wouldn't.'

'And neither would I.' He smiled, and there was amusement in his voice as he said, 'So that's all right, then. We see eye to eye on the fundamentals, which is a healthy start to any relationship. It's good to clear the air, don't you think?'

Clear the air? She didn't answer but she knew she was existing in a thick whirling smog through which she was inching bit by bit without any visible direction. He scared her. He fascinated her and disturbed her and brought all sorts of wild thoughts and emotions to the surface, emotions she would have sworn on oath she was incapable of just weeks ago, but in spite of everything she couldn't expel him from her life. Not yet. She would regret it for ever if she did. This…attraction between them had to run its course and slowly begin to wane, as such things always did. Only then would she be able to put it down to a sharp learning curve about both herself and what was possible in the future.

They had arrived at the house. Travis opened the back of the estate car and the three dogs bounded out, Harvey appearing extremely pleased with himself. The two females had obviously fully accepted him and he was delighted with the canine company.

The rain was coming down in a sheet now, the summer storm suddenly ferocious, and despite it only being a few steps to the front door Beth was dripping water by the time she was standing in the hall. Travis disappeared into the downstairs cloakroom and reappeared with a fluffy towel. 'Here.' He handed it to her, raking back his own wet hair, careless of the shower of droplets. 'I'll put some coffee on, or perhaps you'd prefer a glass of wine?'

She would, actually. She needed something stronger than coffee after seeing Travis damp and sexy, his shirt moulded to his muscled chest and his five o'clock shadow accentuating his virile maleness. 'Wine, please,' she managed shakily.

'Good choice.' He grinned at her and a thousand nerve-endings responded in an orchestra of pure sensation.

Once in the massive kitchen, Beth perched herself on a stool and tried to pretend she was calm and collected as rain hurled itself against the window and thunder rolled ominously overhead. She had never been at her best in a storm but with the three dogs as cool as cucumbers and Travis utterly relaxed and at ease she would rather die than admit to the jitters. Nevertheless, as a particularly savage slash of lightning forked across the sky, she felt herself flinch and immediately the piercing grey eyes were on her face. 'OK?' Travis said mildly.

Beth nodded. 'Fine. It just made me jump, that's all.'

'Summer storms are always the worst. Atmospherics and all that.'

She opened her mouth to agree with him but the words were never voiced as the most tremendous bang she had ever heard shook the windows. She screamed—she couldn't help it—but as the dogs had leapt to their feet and were barking madly her scream was lost in the general mêlée.

Travis had reached her and taken her into his arms in the next moment, his voice soothing as he murmured, 'It's OK, don't panic. I think it's hit something outside, not the house.'

'But it was so loud.' She found she was shaking.

He pushed her back down on the stool and walked to the window, staring out into the wild afternoon as the rain streamed down the glass. 'It's one of the oak trees, by the look of it,' he said after a moment or two. 'Lightning's sliced it in two.'

Beth joined him at the window and as her hand came to her mouth she looked with fascinated horror at what was virtually half a huge tree lying across the lawn, the topmost branches stretched out almost to the house walls. 'Poor thing,' she whispered, her eyes moving to the splintered remains just visible through the deluge. 'It won't recover, will it?'

'It's a major branch, admittedly, that tree forked in two from the trunk, but you'd be amazed at the resilience of nature. I'll get a good tree surgeon in and with a bit of tlc it might rally. Even with the cruellest of blows you don't have to lie down and play dead.'

He wasn't talking about the oak tree any more. Beth stared at him as he turned and looked down into her pale face before folding her into him again.

His kisses were drugging and sweet, his large hands powerfully gentle and wonderfully experienced as he began to please her. Beth was aware of the heat of his fingers through the thin material of the dress, the sensual onslaught slow and lazy but enchantingly erotic.

His tongue rippled along her teeth—Beth shivered. His hands worked magic on her silky skin—she arched helplessly. He let his mouth ease its way to her cheeks, her ears, her throat, his kisses gathering in intensity until they were hot and burningly intoxicating. He was evoking aching pleasure wherever his mouth and hands touched but he took his time, nuzzling into the damp scented shadows of her collarbone as he murmured her name in a smoky voice that sent tremors flooding down to her toes.

The taste, the smell of him spun in her head and she found she couldn't get close enough to him, little whimpers coming from her throat as she clung to the broad width of his shoulders. The desire he was evoking was like a fire inside her, spreading dangerously, and she had no thought of pulling away or trying to stop the spell he'd woven around them. This was a different world, a different universe, and everything else had melted away.

When he gathered her up and began to carry her she knew where they were heading and made no effort to stop him. She could hardly believe it therefore when, instead of making for the stairs as she had imagined, he carried her through to the sprawling oak-beamed sitting room and sat down with her on his lap in one of the deep sofas. But then he was kissing her again and Beth ceased to think. She didn't care where they were as long as he kept holding her.

She found her softness fitted into the hard frame of his male body as though it had been created for that purpose. His kisses and caresses were deeper, hungrier, guided by a controlled assurance of her response. Her body was betraying her need of him just as his arousal confirmed what she was doing to him, his manhood rock-hard and his breathing harsh and guttural. She felt she couldn't get close enough to him.

How long they stayed in the sensual bubble he had created Beth was never sure, but gradually, as the rain abated and the light outside the sitting room windows became bright again, she realised he wasn't going to take things any further. His kisses had become lighter, softer, his hands ceasing their wanderings before he straightened her dress and then rose to his feet still with her in his arms. As he let her gently to the floor her eyes opened, disbelief warring with desire. 'Travis?'

It was a soft confused murmur and for a moment something flared in the grey eyes which made her think he was going to take her upstairs after all. Then a shutter came down, blanking the emotion. 'It's too soon,' he said quietly, answering the unspoken question in her face. 'All this is new to you, isn't it? Your body is telling me so.'

She stiffened, rejection whitening her face. 'I was married for a while,' she reminded him tightly. 'I have made love with a man before.'

'I don't think so.' And, as she went to object, he put a finger on her lips. 'You've been taken by a man before,' he continued very softly, 'but that's not the same thing at all. He didn't take the time to awaken you, to bring you alive. Oh, he probably pleasured you a little—I'm not saying he forced you—but he was more intent on his own pleasure than yours.'

'How can you say that? You don't know Keith; you've never even met him.' For a moment she wondered why she was arguing with him when it had been her who had insisted she didn't want to get involved with him, physically or in any other way. But somehow logic had gone out of the window.

'I know all I need to know about him from how you are.' In contrast to her clipped voice, his was calm and cool. 'He didn't worship you with his body, Beth. He didn't spend hours taking you from one peak of pleasure to the next until you thought you'd die from the ecstasy he was giving you. He didn't spend all night touching and tasting and giving and receiving. He had no real finesse, no wish to learn what you wanted, needed. I know this. And now, for the first time, you are sensing what things can be like between a man and a woman and it's bewitching you.'

He stepped back a pace, his rugged face betraying nothing. 'And that's good.' He smiled a smile which wasn't really a smile at all. 'It's a start. But I want more than your curiosity, sexual or otherwise. So we get to know each other first as we've agreed.'

She thought *she* had been the one who had decided that. Now she wasn't so sure. She stared at him, feeling as if the ground had shifted beneath her feet again just when she had thought she'd reached solid land. And then the old feelings of shame and humiliation and rejection that had come in the aftermath of Keith's betrayal washed over her again. Whatever Travis was saying, however he was dressing it up, he didn't want her, not enough, or he would have taken her when he knew he could have.

'I want you, Beth.' As he had done several times before, he'd read her mind. 'I'll prove how much one day, I promise you. But for now you have to trust me.'

Her eyes flickered and she looked down, but not before he had seen what was in her gaze as his next words confirmed. 'And you're not there yet, are you? So…we wait. Until you understand.'

'Understand what?' The thick smog was back tenfold.

'You'll know one day.' He reached out and took her hand, his firm and warm. 'Let's finish that wine.'

CHAPTER NINE

OVER THE NEXT WEEKS Beth began to think that the more she grew to know Travis the less she understood him, herself too, for that matter. She now accepted he had lured her out of her state of solitude, at least at the weekends. He had introduced her to his friends in the district and Sandra had made an appearance a few times, the two women finding they got on very well.

At the beginning of August, when they had known each other for three months, Travis decided to throw a big party for his thirty-fifth birthday, inviting lots of friends from Bristol and all over the country as well as the Shropshire crowd. Catherine and Michael came too, Beth's sister reaffirming her total approval of Travis several times throughout the weekend.

'He's gorgeous, Neddy. But then you know that, don't you?' Catherine sighed dreamily on the Sunday afternoon when everyone was having a barbecue under a brilliant blue sky, the buzz of conversation and laughter flowing around them as they sat together on a swing seat under the shade of a beech tree.

Yes, Beth said. She knew that.

'I mean he's *everything* a girl could want.' Catherine speared a juicy prawn with her fork and chewed before she added slyly, 'And I bet I was right about the bed thing, wasn't I? He's dynamite, admit it.'

Beth smiled weakly. 'You know I don't kiss and tell.'

'Make an exception. Just this once?'

'Sorry.' Beth filled her mouth with fillet steak.

'I know I was right, anyway.' Catherine grinned at her happily. 'I've seen the way you look at him and he looks at you. You two are *hot.*'

Beth dug her sister in the ribs and they both laughed, but once the weekend was over and she was alone again Beth brooded on their conversation. Catherine wouldn't have believed her if she'd told her sister she hadn't been in Travis's bed yet. No one would believe her. Everyone thought they were a couple in every sense of the word, that much had been obvious from the surprise which she had sensed when she had gone home to the cottage on the Saturday night after the main party.

Not that anyone had actually said anything, of course. They were far too polite and tactful for that, but she had seen their faces and had known exactly what they were thinking. It had embarrassed her, made her feel gauche and awkward. Not so Travis.

Beth frowned to herself. In fact, he had seemed totally unbothered by what anyone thought. Typical man. Or should she say typical Travis? Because Travis was *definitely,* most definitely, not a typical man. Unique didn't even begin to do him justice. She couldn't think of a word that did.

He was a very tactile individual and powerfully experienced in the art of making love, that was for sure, but he always stopped before things progressed too far. To her dismay, several times she had been on the verge of begging him to finish what he'd begun, his kisses and caresses creating such a desire that pride had flown out of the window. But something had stopped her. One little word. Trust. Because if he asked her—as she knew he would—she couldn't give him the answer he wanted. She didn't trust him—she didn't trust any man. She never would again. Emotional suicide wasn't an option.

She sighed so heavily that Harvey came and put his enormous head on her knee, his brown eyes enquiring. They had just finished breakfast and normally she was up and out in the garden or taking him for a walk immediately she'd finished eating. But the weekend had been particularly un-settling, probably because it had emphasised something she had been trying to ignore for a few weeks now. *They couldn't go on the way they were.* It was ridiculous—the whole thing had grown more ridiculous week by week. But they had reached stalemate.

'Walk?' she suggested to Harvey.

The magic word sent him racing to the front door and despite her thoughts Beth had to smile at his exuberance. How Harvey would settle back into the normal routine of London when they had to leave this place she didn't know. A chill settled on her for a moment and then she shrugged. She'd deal with leaving here when she had to. She'd deal with leaving *Travis* when she had to. Day at a time and all that.

Stopping just long enough to fill her small backpack with a couple of bottles of water and a snack for lunch, Beth set off, determined to walk the blues away. It had always worked before and it would work today. She'd make it.

Only it didn't. The bracken-covered hillsides, the odd cottage tucked between orchards and hedgerows, the shining rivers snaking among the trees and hills of every shape and size were just the same as usual. Steep lanes, stone bridges, summits, dark with heather, and quiet fields, they passed them all. But the peace they normally gave her was absent. The scented warm air, Harvey's enjoyment of his surroundings, even the brightly coloured kingfisher Beth spotted on the way home much later failed to thrill.

What was the matter with her? Twilight was falling and she still had a couple of miles to go before the cottage would be in sight, but she sat down on the river bank, Harvey immediately seizing the opportunity to have a drink from the crystal clear water. Tits were chirping in the tree tops and with the gurgle and splashing of the river it should have been a perfect summer evening. It *was* perfect except… She was alone. No, not alone. Lonely. That was different. And she was lonely for just one person.

'No.' She said the word out loud as though it would help to deny what she was feeling. She missed Travis. She had only waved him goodbye the night before but already she missed him. And recently the five days between Sunday evening and Friday, when she would see him again, had seemed to get longer and longer. And it wasn't just the thrill of being in his arms she missed. She missed *him*. His humour, their conversations, their time together, everything. The whole package.

'I don't want this.' Again she spoke out loud but now she could hear the panic in her voice. She didn't want to need him in her life. She had been there once and she couldn't go there again. This was supposed to have been a casual romantic interlude, that was all. She wasn't supposed to have fallen in love. *Fallen in Love?* Where had that come from?

The words reverberated in her head, her surroundings moving to the perimeter of her consciousness. *Love.* She put her hand to her heart, which was thumping so hard it was making her feel ill. She loved him. The knowledge had been staring her in the face for a while but she just hadn't had the courage to acknowledge it. But she did—she loved Travis Black…

She jumped to her feet, calling to Harvey, who came at once, clearly more than ready for home and his dinner. She didn't want to love Travis, she *couldn't* love him. With love came all sorts of complications she could do without.

She walked the rest of the way home slowly, her mind so preoccupied it came as something of a surprise when the cottage came into view, bathed in a serene twilight.

Travis didn't want her to fall in love with him any more than she wanted it, she told herself feverishly a little while later as she fixed Harvey's dinner. Oh, he wanted her friendship and trust, and not least her body, he had made that clear. He wanted them to be on an equal footing emotionally and physically so an affair between them wouldn't leave a bad taste in the mouth when it finally ended. But that was vastly different from love. A million light years away, in fact.

She set Harvey's bowl on the floor and the big dog immediately did a good imitation of a vacuum cleaner as the food disappeared at an amazing rate.

Travis had told her early on in their relationship that he had loved and lost the love of his life, had spelt it out in no uncertain terms, in fact. At the time she hadn't felt he was warning her that his commitment to another woman could only be a limited one—she had been feeling so muddled and confused herself—but maybe it had been a subtle hint to that effect? Yes, thinking about it now, she was sure it had been.

After putting Harvey's bowl in the deep stone sink, Beth made herself a cup of coffee and carried it out into the tiny back garden, which was now dark and still. The scent of roses and white lilies from several of the tubs was heavy in the warm air, the moonlight giving a little light but obscuring any imperfections so that all that remained was perfume and perfect quiet. She could have been the only person in the whole world.

As Harvey dropped himself at her feet, Beth sat on the bench, the wood still retaining the day's heat, and sipped at the fragrant coffee. How had this love crept up on her? she asked herself weakly. When had sexual attraction and fascination changed into something deeper? She couldn't put her finger on a specific point, but changed it had. Perhaps it had been a steady drip drip over the last weeks as he had worked himself into her life, talking to her, revealing so much of himself, making her laugh, making her mad, just being *Travis?*

Could you love someone without trusting them? She frowned in the shadows. Surely love and trust were inseparable companions?

Why question the obvious? her mind retorted. She was living proof of it. She loved him—she loved him so much it frightened her to death and the feeling she'd had for Keith was a pale reflection in comparison, but she didn't trust him. He was a man—a fiercely attractive, powerful, successful man to boot—a man who would only have to snap his fingers to have women lining up. Perhaps if he had been Mr Average, a nine to five, potential family man with no baggage and nothing to set him apart from the crowd, there might have been a chance she could lower her defences enough to risk letting him in.

But Travis was light years away from being Mr Average. The party this weekend had been indicative of how things were. All the men wanted to be like him and all the women, even the happily married ones like Catherine, thought he was drop dead gorgeous and made no bones about it either. When she thought of how many females had been fluttering their eyelashes at him…

What was this woman like who had spurned his love? She found herself clutching the coffee cup so tightly she was in danger of snapping the china handle and forced herself to relax her grip. How could *any* woman walk away from a man like Travis? Especially if he loved her? She bit down hard on her lip before drinking the rest of the coffee and then continuing to sit in darkness. The normal peace it gave her was absent, however.

It was the ringing of her mobile phone in her bag which she had left in the kitchen which brought her to her feet a few minutes later. As she walked into the house she glanced at her watch. Eleven o'clock. Bit late for Catherine. Her heart began to thud. Travis had begun the habit of ringing her last thing lately, once or twice a week. Up until now she had refused to acknowledge she'd begun to be disappointed on the nights he didn't call.

'Hello, Beth.' His voice was deep and warm. 'I haven't woken you, have I? I know it's a little late to call.'

'No, I was sitting in the garden having a coffee.' Considering the way her heart was careering around her breast cavity Beth thought she'd done quite well to answer so normally. 'Anything wrong?' she added carefully.

'Plenty.' It was wry. 'The main thing being I'm in Bristol and you're in Shropshire.' There was a pause which Beth found herself utterly unable to break. Then he said, very softly, 'Missing me? Wishing I was with you?'

So much. Forcing lightness into her voice, Beth said, 'You only left late last night.'

'That wasn't what I asked.'

She shut her eyes tightly. They indulged in such banter often these days but now, with her new knowledge of her love for him, she couldn't play the game. She knew she had been playing with fire for months now. She should have realised it wasn't a matter of *if* she would get burnt, only when. She had thought she'd experienced the lowest point of her life when Keith had betrayed her so badly. She had been wrong. Sending Travis out of her life was going to be much worse. But it had to be done. For both their sakes.

She took a deep silent breath and prayed for the right words. He must never know the power he had over her. Keith hadn't been able to break her but Travis would. Not that he would want to—she didn't believe he was a bad person, far from it— but everything that could be wrong for them as a couple *was* wrong. She would never know a moment's peace if she became his woman in every sense of the word. Right from the first time they slept together she would be waiting for him to tire of her and go on to the next female who threw herself at him. And they would. They did.

'Beth?' His voice was still warm but she detected a shadow of wariness. 'What's the matter?'

'Nothing's the matter.' She wished she'd had something stronger than coffee to give her Dutch courage for what she was about to do. 'I was going to call you tomorrow, actually. I wanted you to be the first to hear what I've decided to do. I'm feeling so much better I think it's time to get back to work, take up all the strings again.'

There was a brief silence. 'I see.' It was steady and expressionless. 'I thought you wanted to stay at the cottage for a full six months. Wasn't that the plan?'

'I did at first.' She swallowed. 'But, as I said, I feel fine now and…and it's a bit boring here some-times.' She tried to inject a note of truth into the lie.

The silence was even longer. 'We'll talk about this at the weekend,' he said finally. 'OK?'

Not OK. She knew it was cowardly but if she saw him again she would be terrified of what she might reveal. This had to be a clean swift severing of all contact. She opened her mouth to say she would be gone by the weekend but then something stopped her. Travis was quite capable of driving straight up to see her. In fact she was sure he would do that. They had become close in the last months, much too close. He would expect more than a long distance finish to their relationship—as he had every right to, she admitted miserably. If anyone else did what she was planning to do, she'd consider them the lowest of the low. But she couldn't bear seeing him again.

'Beth?' Again he prompted her, his voice now carrying a note of concern which made her feel even more of a worm. 'Has something happened? Are you all right?'

No, she wasn't all right. She would never be all right again in the whole of her life. Why had he made her love him? How could she have been so foolish as to think she could handle this in the first place? 'I'm fine,' she said flatly.

'You don't sound fine.' The tone was grim.

She took refuge in the universal get-out clause. 'I've got a headache, that's all. It's the hot weather.'

'A headache.' Travis being Travis, he didn't even try to pretend he believed her. 'Taken anything for it?' he asked sceptically. 'Aspirin, paracetamol?'

'Of course.' She grimaced at the phone. How did he always know when she was lying? He was a human lie detector.

'I'll get off the phone and leave you to get to

bed, then. Goodnight, Beth.' It was abrupt, cold. 'Sleep tight.'

He didn't even wait for her to reply before he finished the call. Beth blinked. No sweet nothings. No trying to persuade her to open up. Not that she would have, of course, but he might at least have *tried*.

She stood in the kitchen, her stomach churning. She was a headcase. He had turned her into a headcase. And then her innate honesty made her add, no, that wasn't fair. The blame for this couldn't be laid at Travis's feet.

One good cry later and ten minutes of pacing the cottage brought her to the point of calling Travis back before she stopped halfway into the number. She didn't even get as far as halfway the second and third times.

It was gone two before she finally crawled into bed and the dratted owl hooted her into four o'clock still wide awake. She must have fallen asleep some time after that because when the knocking at the front door woke her bright sunlight was spilling into the room.

'Good morning.' Travis looked like an advertisement for some designer or other, his pale suit and midnight-blue shirt impeccable and his black hair glinting in the sunshine.

Beth stared at him stupidly, trying to form

coherent speech out of the cottonwool muddle of her mind.

'Can I come in?' he asked with some coolness.

'Oh, yes, yes, come in.' She stood aside and let him pass her, doing her best to ignore what the smell of delicious limey aftershave on clean male skin was doing to her hormones. As she shut the front door she managed to say, 'What are you doing here?' realising that should have been her opening line.

'Seeing you.' He didn't smile. Neither had he brought any croissants or goodies today, she noticed, her heart beginning to thump. 'I get the impression we need to talk.'

'What time is it?' She glanced helplessly at the clock on the wall above the fireplace. Eight o'clock. He must have been up at the crack of dawn. 'Coffee?' she offered weakly, clicking her fingers at Harvey, who as always had given Travis a rapturous welcome.

'Thanks.' It was polite but disinterested.

'I'll just let Harvey out first.' She opened the front door again and let the big dog out for his normal nose around the front garden, before walking through to the kitchen where she made them both a quick mug of instant coffee.

Travis was standing in exactly the same place when she returned. He still wasn't smiling.

He took the coffee with a nod, refusing her invitation to be seated. He waited until she had sat down on the sofa before he spoke. 'So?' The grey eyes were piercing. 'What is this all about, Beth? Let's have it.'

No attempt to kiss or hug her. A large fat bumble bee which had flown in when she had opened the door for Harvey buzzed angrily against the window before settling on a pot plant. The stillness was profound.

'This?' she prevaricated, hating herself for her cowardice. But with Travis in front of her the courage of the night before was only a memory. She should have just disappeared this week.

'Correct me if I'm wrong, but when you spoke of leaving it wasn't only Shropshire you had in mind. Right?'

'I didn't say that.' She stared at him helplessly.

'But it's what you meant,' he persisted grimly.

She could fob him off. Make up some excuse. Deflect what was clearly going to be one awful mess of a goodbye. 'Yes.' She raised her eyes from the coffee. 'I did mean that. I...I think it's going to be simpler if we call it a day now.'

'Simpler?' The grey was granite-hard. 'For whom?'

'For both of us,' she said a little desperately. 'We...we've had fun and it's been great, but once

I'm back in London it would be too difficult to keep seeing each other. The distance—'

'Is nothing,' he interrupted icily. 'And you know it.'

He was looking straight at her but she couldn't determine what he was thinking. His expression was closed, devoid of emotion, like a poker player determined to give nothing away. She suddenly realised what had made him such a successful businessman. He would be a formidable opponent.

'Of course it is,' she argued miserably. 'Long distance relationships always go wrong.'

'We're not talking continents, Beth, merely a few miles between one city and another. So let's cut the excuses and get to the chase. I thought everything was going well between us—great, in fact. What changed overnight? Did anyone upset you at the weekend? Say something? What?'

Her throat felt dry and the coffee didn't ease it when she took a few sips. She pulled her robe tighter round her. 'Can't you just accept it's better if we call it a day now?'

'No, Beth, I can't.' His body was very still, very controlled. 'You are going to talk to me for once. Open up that damn closed box in your mind. We both know there have been times when I could have taken you and you would have been willing. You're not the sort of woman to do that lightly. We were getting somewhere. It was good. I thought—' He stopped abruptly.

'What?' she said faintly.

He waved an impatient hand. 'Never mind. This isn't about me, it's about you. So what has put us back to square one? What went so wrong that you were going to creep off without even giving me the courtesy of an explanation?'

He had known. She didn't bother to deny it, her beetroot-red face was confirmation enough if he had needed it. Which he obviously didn't. She wanted to break the hold his eyes had on hers but she couldn't. 'I…I told you at the beginning how things stood with me. I didn't come here looking for a relationship—'

'But then you met me,' he interrupted with magnificent arrogance. 'And everything changed.'

She averted her face at last, dragging her gaze from his as she finished the coffee. Her throat ached as she swallowed. She didn't want to hurt him, she told herself frantically, but at least it was only his pride that would take a fall. This might dent his ego but it wasn't as if he loved her or anything like that. In a few weeks, a few days even, she would be replaced. He might even meet someone who *could* supplant his lost love.

She ignored the blinding pain that thought brought in its wake, her voice hollow as she said,

'I can't be what you want me to be, Travis. You must know that by now. Deep inside.'

He swore, softly but savagely, and for a moment the mask slipped. 'I don't want you to be anything other than yourself. I never have. I thought I had made that perfectly clear.'

'You want me to trust you,' she stated flatly.

'Is that so big a deal?'

'Yes, for me.' She was shouting now but she didn't care. 'It's the biggest thing in the world, if you want to know. And I can't do it. It's as simple as that. I can't trust you.'

'Wrong.' In comparison he was deadly calm. 'You *won't* do it. There's a difference.'

'Can't, won't, whatever.' Her whole body was trembling.

Again he swore but this time it was exasperation rather than fury. When he walked over to the sofa and raised her up into his arms Beth didn't have the will to resist. But he didn't try to make love to her as she had expected. Instead he merely held her close against the strong shield of his body, his voice soft above her head as he said, 'Why are you doing this to yourself right now, sweetheart? There are no time limits except in your mind; surely you know that.'

It was the 'sweetheart' that did it. She could have withstood his contempt or anger but not the tender quality to the endearment. It pierced the last of her control. Tears spilled over on to her cheeks and she wrenched herself away, covering her face with her hands as she sobbed. 'Go, please go. I don't want you here. This has to end now. Please, Travis.'

He made no attempt to hold her again but his voice was inflexible when he stated, 'I am not leaving, Beth.'

'Please.' She had never felt such pain, such hopelessness.

'No.' And then she was in his arms again. 'Not until I've talked sense into that crazy head of yours. I'm not going to let what that fool of an ex-husband of yours did ruin both our lives. These last weeks you've been happy, I know you have. OK, I might not be perfect but I know when something is right or wrong, and we are right together. Perhaps I shouldn't have waited, perhaps I should have taken you to bed weeks ago, but that can be remedied right now. But first I want to tell you something. I wanted to wait, give you more time to get used to having someone in your life again, but you've forced the issue. I don't want an affair with you, Beth. I never have. I've had enough open-ended relationships to know when the real thing hits.'

'What?' She couldn't take it in. She heard what

he was saying but the words were all jumbled in her mind and she couldn't make sense of them.

He held her away from him slightly, the grey eyes narrowing as they fastened on her face, which was now chalk-white. 'I love you,' he said simply. 'I fell in love with you the first moment I saw you when you were standing in the dark in those ridiculous pink pyjamas covered in dirt and goodness knows what. I want to marry you, Beth. I want to wake up beside you in bed every morning for the rest of my life.'

'No.' She felt numb. 'No, you can't love me. You said you had lost the woman you loved. You said that.'

His gaze had sharpened and she knew her reaction to his declaration was not what he'd hoped for. 'I think I said the woman I loved didn't feel the same as I did,' he said slowly. 'That's not the same.'

'But…but you let me believe…'

She couldn't go on but he knew what she was trying to say anyway. 'It would have scared you to death and certainly back to London if I had told you how I felt at that point. Hell, it scared me, if you want to know. It still does.'

'But you didn't know me, not really, not then.' This couldn't be true. 'Love at first sight is just a fantasy, everyone knows that. It can't happen in real life.'

'I knew you in my soul before time, that's the only way I can explain it. And, before you protest, if anyone else had told me I'd be saying this just months ago I'd have laughed in their face. I was enjoying my life, I didn't want to fall in love, didn't want to have to consider anyone else. I liked a lifestyle where I was answerable to no one and as free as a bird. But all that changed in one moment.'

'Travis.' It was a strangled sound. 'Please, don't say any more…'

'I've walked on eggshells for the last three months, Beth. I'm done with it. You tell me you're prepared to walk away from what we have so I've nothing to lose in calling a spade a spade now, have I? I *love* you, dammit!'

His voice had risen but almost immediately he gained control. 'I love you,' he repeated softly. 'And, whatever you say, I don't believe you're completely indifferent to me. You have changed in the last few weeks, let your guard down. I've been aware of it even if you haven't. I won't let you finish this because you have tarred all men with the same brush. However bad it was at the end with Keith, you have to face up to the fact that you can't exist in a bubble.'

'You don't understand.' Beth lifted her face but she could hardly see him through a haze of tears.

'No, I don't. I won't pretend I do. I haven't

been married before, committed my life to someone only to be let down in the worst possible way. But I have loved someone and lost them. I do know what grief is. Kirk taught me about that.'

'I…I lost my parents so I know what you mean, but this is something completely different.'

He stared at her and now she saw anger colouring the clear grey. It was in his voice when he spoke, the tone grim. 'Yes, it's different but it's about time you finished with the self-pity and thinking the world only revolves around you.'

Beth was shocked to the core. Never, in all the time they had been together, had he spoken or looked like this.

'People go through worse than you have,' he continued when she didn't answer him. 'And I'm not demeaning what you suffered either. But you came out the other side, you survived. Maybe hanging on by your fingertips, but you survived. Do you mean to tell me that was all for nothing? That you are going to let this cretin have the last laugh? Where's the backbone that got you through the divorce?'

'How dare you speak to me like this?' Anger dispelled the numbness of shock, her eyes blazing. 'How *dare* you?'

'Because I love you, that's why. Maybe it would have been better if we'd met a few years later.

Eighteen months isn't long to come to terms with it all, I know that, but we didn't. That's life. Neat packages are an illusion.'

'I want you to leave.'

'Tough. I want a lot of things but it doesn't look as if I'm getting them either,' Travis responded grimly.

Beth fought for composure as she stood up and faced him. 'This is my home, albeit temporarily, and you're not welcome any more,' she said, the brief support of anger dying and leaving her terrified. She couldn't weaken—she mustn't. He said he loved her, and perhaps he did, but it didn't alter the fact that Travis was the man with it all. How could she, Beth Marton, ever hope to hang on to a man like him? She didn't have what it took, she knew that. She was ordinary, nothing special. All over the country other women, plain or pretty, fat or thin, managed to make their marriages work but hers had failed amid devastation. If she hadn't been enough for Keith, how could she ever hope to be enough for Travis?

'You don't believe I love you?' Travis's face was rigid, slashes of colour across the hard cheekbones.

'You perhaps think you do.' Her voice was unsteady, anguished. 'In fact I'm sure you believe you do.'

'But you're not sure.' His features had softened.

'So we go on as before until you are sure. Do you think you could ever love me?' he added quietly. 'I shouldn't ask, but…'

Beth averted her face. The night she had walked out on Keith was something of a blur in her mind, so much had been said—screamed even—and she had been so distraught. But one thing was crystal clear. Amid all the accusations and counter-accusations, the lying by Keith and the pain and bewilderment she had been feeling, she had asked him why he had done this thing to her. Why, when he had said he loved her, married her, had he continued to see Anna and the other women?

He had looked at her and said what was possibly the only honest statement he'd voiced that night. 'Because I could. Because you let me. You never queried anything I said. Never challenged me when I was late or went away on business trips. You took everything at face value from when we met.'

And when she had cried that was because she had loved him, trusted him with every fibre of her being, he had stared at her for a moment before shrugging. Even then, she knew, he had been confident of his power over her, had been convinced he would be able to talk her round. And she had given him that power in the beginning by loving him, by telling him every day how much she adored him, by believing in him and closing her eyes and her reason to any question marks which had cropped up during their twelve months of marriage. It had almost destroyed her. She raised her face, her heart hammering in frightened, panicked beats. This time when she lied he had to believe her.

'No,' she said very steadily. 'I couldn't love you.'

She saw the blood drain from his face and for one awful moment was close to flinging herself on him and begging him to forgive her, to admitting she loved him more than she had thought possible, that he was everything she'd ever wanted in a man. A paralysing fear stopped her. The same emotion enabled her to stand as still as stone when he nodded slowly.

There was an unnerving silence, vibrating with terrifying intensity, before he said tonelessly, 'Then there really is nothing more to be said, after all. Goodbye, Beth.'

She watched in numb disbelief as he turned on his heel and strode across to the front door, opening it without looking back. Harvey had bounded in and then, as Travis closed the door behind him, whined and pawed at it as though to ask what was happening.

It wasn't until she heard the car start that Beth came to life. Without thinking, she ran across the room and flung open the door, calling his name. The car was already out of sight. Shouting, she stumbled across the garden to the gate, Harvey barking anxiously at the side of her, but it was too late. He had gone. And she knew this time he wouldn't be coming back.

CHAPTER TEN

'YOU DID WHAT?' Catherine stared at her, utterly aghast.

'I finished with Travis,' Beth repeated flatly. 'Yesterday morning. It's over, *really* over.'

'But why? I thought everything was going so well. I mean...' Catherine ran out of words to express what she meant and instead collapsed on a kitchen stool.

Beth had knocked at her sister's door five minutes before and, James being upstairs in his cot for his morning nap, had decided to get the confession over and done with. She had let Catherine assume she had travelled down to London for a quick visit until her sister had made the coffee and they had a plate of chocolate biscuits in front of them. Then she had broken the news. It had gone down like a lead balloon.

'And,' she said now, 'I've moved back into my flat. Last night. So, life as normal.'

Catherine was looking at her as though she was mad and Beth couldn't really blame her. She felt she was *going* mad.

'Life as normal?' Catherine shook her head, her fair hair swinging disapprovingly. 'Life without Travis, you mean?'

Hearing it put like that was like a punch in the stomach. But she deserved it. She deserved much worse, Beth thought miserably. She was the biggest coward out and she knew it. Travis had said as much and she agreed with him. *Travis.* Oh, Travis. She could hardly believe she wouldn't see him again.

'What did he do wrong?' Catherine took a sip of her coffee, her eyes narrowing on Beth's pale face and pink-rimmed eyes.

'He asked me to marry him,' Beth said woodenly.

Catherine gave a squeak and sat bolt upright. 'And that's it? Not even you would be so stupid. What else happened?'

'It's complicated.' Or terribly simple. She wasn't sure.

'Knowing you, it would be,' Catherine said with sisterly frankness. 'But do I take it he didn't cheat or turn violent or confess to being an axe-murderer?'

'Of course he didn't.' Beth reared up at the possibility.

'So basically the guy tells you he loves you and

you dump him. Yes? He bares his heart and you show him the door?'

'I told him I wanted to end it before he told me he loved me,' Beth said flatly, knowing it was no defence.

'Oh, that's all right, then.' Catherine glared at her. 'You've just dumped a guy in a million for what reason, Beth? I mean, tell me, because I'd really like to know.'

'You're not making this easy.' Actually Catherine's antagonism was easier to deal with than sympathy. Sympathy would have had her howling like James in one of his tantrums, especially as she knew she didn't merit any.

'Good reason for that.' Catherine bit into a chocolate biscuit with enough force to reduce it to spraying fragments. 'I think you're stark staring mad. Especially because you like him, don't you? And don't deny it, I know you do.'

'I wasn't going to deny it.' She needed someone to talk to and family fitted the bill. Perhaps.

'Hmm.' Catherine fixed her with a big sister frown. 'Is that like him or *really* like him?' she pressed.

Beth just looked at her, her expression answer enough.

'So why did you finish with him, then?' Catherine asked vehemently. 'Beth, this is madness.'

'Because it wouldn't work,' Beth said miserably.

'Says who? It was working pretty well from where I was standing. He loves you, you love him. He's talking marriage, for goodness' sake. What's not to work?'

'Catherine, it's not like you think.' Beth rubbed at her eyes, which hadn't recovered from the marathon of weeping and were sore and smarting. 'We…we hadn't actually slept together, for a start. Not that Travis didn't want to,' she added quickly in case Catherine got the wrong idea, 'but I said at the beginning I needed more time before anything like that and he promised to take it at my pace. I…'

She didn't know how to put this. She rubbed at her eyes again and then decided to just say it. 'I love him but I can't take the risk of it all falling apart again. I'm not ready for a relationship, let alone marriage. I don't think I ever will be. It's not how I see the future.'

Catherine said an extremely rude word. 'It's him, Keith, isn't it?' she growled. 'You're letting him influence how you think about things. For crying out loud, Beth. Travis isn't Keith. Surely you can see that? How can you let Keith ruin any chance of happiness in the future?'

'That's what Travis said.' Beth stared at her sister.

'He's right.' Catherine jerked her head in agreement.

'Travis also said it was about time I finished with self-pity and that people have gone through worse than I did.'

'Did he?' Catherine looked impressed. 'I think he's right again but I wouldn't have dared say it.'

So much for blood ties. And this was taking the no sympathy attitude too far. Feeling extremely hard done by, Beth stood up. 'So basically he's right and I'm wrong and I've ruined it all?' she said, her voice wobbly.

Catherine gave a school-marm nod. 'But I'm amazed, knowing Travis, that he accepted it was over. If he loves you and you love him, I would have thought he's the sort of man to fight tooth and nail. I'd have bet my life he's no quitter.'

'He…he doesn't know I love him,' Beth admitted flatly.

'He doesn't?' Catherine raised her eyebrows. 'You haven't told him? Not even when he said how he felt?'

Worse than that. 'I said I didn't love him, actually. When he asked.' Beth waited for the explosion. It didn't happen.

For once Beth had the satisfaction of seeing her sister speechless but in the circumstances it wasn't enjoyable. After a moment or two Catherine said, 'Ring him. Ring him and tell him how you feel. Go for it, girl.'

It was the same thought which had occurred at fairly regular intervals—every thirty seconds, in fact—since Tuesday morning. But always harsh reality followed. 'I can't.' Beth reached for her bag. 'Because the same reasons I finished it still apply. I love him but I don't trust him, Catherine, and I can't help it. I want to trust him but every time I think of the future doubts pour in. And that isn't fair on him. It wouldn't be fair on anyone. You remember what that girl was like we used to know—Christine Brown? After her fiancé jilted her she ruined every relationship that followed with her jealousy.'

'Christine Brown was a headcase.'

'No, she was just massively insecure because of what had occurred. It coloured her relationships. It happens.'

'She was massively insecure *and* a headcase,' Catherine said drily. 'You're not like her. Not remotely.'

'But I might be, with Travis. I love him so much I couldn't bear it if it went bad. At least this way the memories are good, apart from the last meeting, obviously.' That had been as bad as it got.

'Memories don't keep you warm at night,' Catherine said practically. 'Beth, you can't tell me you don't want to settle down at some point in the future. Have children. Can you imagine doing that with anyone other than Travis if you love him like you say you do? You've *always* wanted babies.'

This baring the soul wasn't all it was cut out to be. As the pain sliced through her, Beth turned on her heel. 'I have to go,' she said unsteadily. 'Harvey's been on his own at the flat for an hour or so and I need to take him for a walk.'

'How is he?' Catherine followed her to the front door, her pretty face creased with worry.

'Sulking, more for Travis than the cottage, I think.' Beth tried to smile but it didn't work. Instead her lip quivered.

Catherine gazed at her. 'I wish Mum and Dad were here,' she said with a break in her voice. 'They would have known what to say. I'm getting it all wrong. Making it worse.'

'Oh, Cath, of course you aren't.' Now she was making everyone within a twenty mile radius feel as miserable as her. Beth hugged her sister and they clung together for some moments. When finally they parted both their faces were wet.

'Do something for me.' Catherine stared at her, an I'm-going-to-say-this-even-though-I-know-you'll-hate-it look on her face.

'What?' Beth said warily, blowing her nose.

'Go and see Keith,' Catherine said very firmly.

'*What?*' It was the last thing—the very last

thing—she had expected her sister to say. 'Are you mad? Why on earth would I go and see Keith? I don't even want to breathe the same air.'

'To lay ghosts that won't go away any other way. You haven't seen him since that night you walked out and I think that's a mistake. There was so much happening around that time, Neddy. Mum and Dad going so suddenly, that awful court case and then Anna turning up on your doorstep. If you had gone for counselling after the divorce instead of working night and day you might have had your head sorted by now.'

'I didn't need counselling,' Beth said vehemently.

'Yes, you did.' Catherine wagged her finger at her in a way which was reminiscent of their childhood.

Beth had the same impulse she'd had then to stick out her tongue and make a rude face. Instead she said, 'I know you're trying to be helpful—'

'So listen to me for once,' Catherine interrupted. 'And I'll tell you something now—I never did like Keith. He was too smarmy, too nice, buttering up Mum and Dad and always saying the right thing. He would never have told you people had it worse than you and that you were self-pitying.'

'Cath, I don't want to make contact with Keith. I don't even know where he is. I don't *care* where he is!'

'Try his work first; he's probably still in the

same job. If not, you know where Anna lives. Go and see her. Or see if he's living in the same place.'

'You're not listening to me,' Beth said, her face tight.

'No, *you're* not listening to *me,*' Catherine counter-attacked. 'And, as we've both agreed you're a headcase and I'm not, I think you should. Apart from the fact I'm your big sister, I'm a very logical and sane person. Frankly, what have you got to lose, Neddy? At least promise me you'll think about going to see him. If you think about it you'll see it makes sense.'

Beth opened the front door. 'OK,' she said flatly. 'I'll think about it. But it doesn't make sense and I won't go.'

She thought about it all the way home through the nightmare of London traffic and, once she'd collected Harvey, during their walk in Hyde Park. She thought about it all evening at the flat, trying to ignore how alien the place felt and how restless Harvey was. She was still thinking about it the next morning after a sleepless night.

She wasn't conscious that she had come to a decision until she found herself dialling Keith's work number. It was a direct line and he answered almost immediately. 'Keith Wright.'

For a second Beth almost dropped the phone. A huge flood of feeling swept through her but she breathed deeply, her voice remarkably steady as she said, 'Hello, Keith. It's Beth.'

'Beth?' The blank astonishment in his voice was clear. And then, after a pause, he said, 'Beth, how wonderful to hear from you,' and now he had switched to the tone he'd always used with her—warm, soft, charming. 'How are you?'

'Fine.' Another deep breath and she was able to say, 'I wondered if you fancied meeting for a coffee at lunchtime.'

'Absolutely. That'd be great.'

There had been no hesitation but then there wouldn't be, would there? Beth thought cynically. An ex-wife added to his ongoing list of conquests would be a feather in his cap as far as he was concerned. She wondered if he would ask why she wanted to see him after all this time. He didn't.

'How about Bailey's?' he suggested smoothly. 'You used to love their *chocolat prélat* cake, remember? In the old days?'

It seemed a lifetime away since she had used to meet him in their lunch hours at Bailey's, a smart little coffee bar that served wonderful sandwiches and desserts as well as every coffee under the sun. 'OK.' She glanced at her watch. 'Twelve o'clock suit you?' It had been their custom to take an early lunch to be sure of getting a table; Bailey's filled to overflowing around one o'clock.

'Twelve would be great, Beth. I'll look forward to it.'

'See you then.' Beth put down the phone before he could continue the conversation and sat staring into space for a few moments. How did she feel? After the brief shock of hearing his voice, remarkably composed, but of course it would be different facing her ex-husband in the flesh.

She sat musing for some time, trying to work out exactly what she wanted from their meeting. She wasn't sure. Catherine had talked about laying ghosts and maybe she was right, but would it be counter-productive to see Keith after all these months? He had made her feel like the biggest fool in the world, the humiliation and pain easier to deal with than feeling she was a complete failure as a woman and a wife. She hadn't been enough for him and, despite the fact she knew Anna and all the others were in the same boat, it hadn't helped. Was she setting herself up for a gigantic fall in meeting him?

She wandered into the bedroom, opening her wardrobe and staring at her clothes without really seeing them. Travis had told her to get some backbone and come out of the protective bubble she'd been existing in. She was seeing Keith today because in her heart of hearts she knew the only way to go forward was to put the past behind her, and she couldn't do that without this one last meeting. She didn't know what it would produce, but it had to be done. End of story.

After taking Harvey for a quick walk to a small park nearby—for which he showed his disgust by refusing to look at her once they were home—she tried to make up for the change in his surroundings by giving him a big bowlful of chicken mixed with his dog meal for breakfast. He ate the food but continued with the sulk and Beth left him to it. She had more important things to focus on.

By eleven o'clock, when she inspected herself in the mirror, she was satisfied with what she saw. The pretty Empire-line dress in a vibrant bold print brought out the golden quality of her tan and made her glow with health. She had left her hair loose, its natural highlights emphasising the silky blondeness and making her blue eyes larger. She'd used the barest minimum of make-up, partly because she didn't want Keith to think she was trying too hard but also because the weeks of tramping the Shropshire countryside under a hot English sun had given her skin a colour no amount of cosmetics could improve. To her great surprise, especially considering how she felt inside, she looked like a confident, proud and beautiful young woman with the world at her feet.

'How the mirror can lie.' She pulled a face at

herself and then turned away. But, as long as she gave Keith the impression all was well, nothing else mattered. She was going to finish this on her terms, exit his life with a bang and not a whimper. She owed herself that.

She arrived at Bailey's dead on twelve o'clock and Keith was already sitting at a table for two in what had once been their favourite spot. A young couple had entered the coffee bar in front of her and he didn't see her immediately, giving her time to study him. As she walked towards him she thought, he's not nearly as handsome as I remember him. Why didn't I see how weak his mouth looks before? How weak and almost pretty his whole face is? He's as unlike Travis as it's possible to be. A tinsel and glitter man, nothing more.

And then he saw her, his mouth breaking into the easy smile which had captured her heart in the old days but now did absolutely nothing for her. *Nothing*.

'Beth.' He had risen to his feet with the good manners she had once thought were natural but now knew were all part of the cultivated charm. 'You look wonderful,' he said smoothly.

'Thank you.' She smiled, avoiding physical contact by sliding into her seat at once. She didn't return the compliment.

'I don't need to ask you how you are,' he continued when he'd sat down himself, and now there was definitely an element of pique that he couldn't quite hide in his manner. She saw him glance at her left hand and it prepared her for his next question. 'Are you with anyone?' he asked in the faintly wistful tone he'd used in the past which had never failed to melt her.

'Yes, I am.' Well, she should be, she told herself, and even if Travis hadn't existed she would have said the same at this moment. 'And you? How are Anna and the children?'

He stared at her as though he couldn't quite believe it was her. But then she didn't feel like the Beth he had known any more, she realised with a great surge of joy. She had moved on. She had *really* moved on from all of this sordid mess.

It was a moment or two before he pulled himself together enough to say, 'Anna doesn't live in England any more. She met someone—I understand she's married now. They live in the States. Michigan, I think. Somewhere like that.'

'And the children?' Beth asked quietly.

'With their mother.' His mouth had thinned and for a second she almost felt sorry for him. Almost. Travis had been right, Keith would end up a lonely old man.

It was on the tip of her tongue to say she was glad for Anna because she genuinely was, but it might look as if she was crowing. Instead she took a sip of the coffee he had ordered in her absence, along with a slice of *chocolat prélat,* and then asked him about his work.

She kept the conversation on general lines throughout the few minutes it took to finish the coffee. The slice of cake she left untouched. And then she stood up, reaching across and holding out her hand as she said, 'Goodbye, Keith. I'm moving away so there will be no chance we'll meet again. I hope you find what you're looking for.'

He was so taken aback he didn't move for some seconds, then he mumbled, 'You're not going already? I thought... I mean, why did you call me?'

Beth smiled. 'To close the old chapter of my life so I can enter the new one with all my heart. You know me, it's all or nothing. I can't function any other way.'

He took her hand, his handshake limp. It fitted somehow. 'Who...who is he?' he muttered resentfully.

'No one you know.' Her smiled widened. 'Goodbye.'

And she walked out of the coffee bar into the bright sunlight, the crushing weight which had been on her shoulders for the last eighteen months gone. It was heady, euphoric, and she knew she was grinning like the Cheshire cat because of the strange looks passers-by were giving her, although one or two smiled tentatively back in return. Bless 'em.

She had been stupid, so stupid, she thought as she walked on, but she had never really cut the last ties which had held her to Keith. Maybe not letting go completely had all been mixed up with her parents dying and the fact that she had really meant every one of her wedding vows, but she couldn't allow a weak, immoral and flawed man to ruin the rest of her life. Travis was the antithesis of Keith in every way and she had to trust in that or she'd be hung up on her past for ever.

A clever, conscienceless liar would always have a certain amount of power over good honest people—was it Travis who had said that? But such power wouldn't and couldn't last because eventually lies were exposed. Keith didn't stand up to the light of day—literally, she thought—because she had noticed the lines appearing round his eyes and mouth and the way his jowls were beginning to hang. Soon those boyish good looks which were a large part of his charm would be gone, and his shallowness would become more and more apparent.

Travis, on the other hand, would stride into old age as virile and magnetic as ever, perhaps even more so because his type of rugged attractiveness lent itself to the ageing process.

She hailed a passing taxi cab and, once she was on her way home, relaxed against the seat. Travis had told her she was the love of his life, that he would never love anyone else and that he wanted to marry her. He had been unbelievably patient with her from the very first whilst still forcing her to face her gremlins and conquer them. He was everything in the world she had ever wanted and she had told him she didn't love him and had sent him away.

Would he forgive her? She shivered in spite of the warm day. And how had she thought she could ever live the rest of her life without him? What was she going to do?

CHAPTER ELEVEN

BY EVENING TIME Beth knew exactly what she was going to do. She had told Keith she was an all or nothing girl and it was true. She had made a mistake of momentous proportions in refusing Travis; only an equally momentous act of repentance would do. She had to show him she meant what she said when she told him she loved him, that she had loved him for some time but had been too scared, and too stubborn, to admit it. It was all the eggs in the basket time.

The next morning she phoned John Turner dead on the dot of nine o'clock. 'John? It's Beth,' she said, after his secretary put her through. 'Have you re-let Herb Cottage yet?'

'Good gracious, no. You'd paid the six months' rent in advance so there was no hurry as far as the owner's concerned. Why?'

'I'm coming back.' She waited silently for his reaction.

'Right.' A pause followed. 'How long for?' he asked carefully. 'Do you intend to see out the rental period?'

Beth got the idea he thought she was a crazy woman and she couldn't blame him. When she had given the keys over she had been adamant she wouldn't be back and that they could re-let at once. 'For the rest of the time and possibly a further six months if the cottage will be available. I'm…I'm selling up in London. I shall be looking for work in your area.'

'I see. I thought—' He stopped abruptly. 'Does Travis know?' he asked after an uncomfortable moment or two.

Obviously the Shropshire grapevine had been active. He clearly was aware there was some sort of trouble between them. 'He will shortly.' Beth hoped he'd leave it at that.

'Right.' There was a longer pause before he said, 'Travis is a good man, Beth. I'd hate to see him messed about.'

'So would I, John,' Beth said softly.

The next telephone call was to the practice where she was employed. After speaking to the senior partner, who was wonderfully understanding, Beth confirmed she would send in a written resignation and he promised her a glowing reference in return.

She wasn't too concerned about that, but she thanked him and they parted amicably. The sale of her flat would mean she was financially independent for a long time, even if she did not secure another job immediately, but she was quite prepared to work at something else—in a shop, helping out at a pub, anything—until the right professional position came along. In fact, she thought she'd rather enjoy it.

Later that afternoon she put the sale of the flat into the hands of the estate agent who had sold it to her. Then she phoned her sister and explained what she was doing. When she had recovered her power of speech, Catherine offered to store any of the furniture and possessions Beth wanted to keep in her spare room and one half of her double garage.

All the immediate wheels set in motion, Beth sat looking out of the flat window over city rooftops as the sky changed from bright blue to dusky mauve streaked with pink. John had promised to drop the cottage key under the plant pot before he went home that night and her bags were packed.

She looked round the flat one last time. Harvey, who had sensed something was afoot and was acting as though he was on springs, whined at her feet. 'One last thing,' she told the big dog quietly. 'The most important thing. Keep your paws crossed for me, Harvey.'

She dialled Travis's mobile number, her heart thumping so hard it hurt. Each ring seemed like a lifetime but then his voice, deep and smoky rich, came over the line. It was a recorded message and, to her surprise, she burst into tears.

Several tissues later, she tried again, and this time managed to wait for the beep. 'It's Beth, Travis. I need to talk to you. I'm sorry, I'm so sorry, I've been such a fool. You're right, people have gone through much worse than I did and I have been self-pitying and all sorts of things. Can you ever forgive me? I shall understand if you can't.' She took a deep breath. 'No, no, I won't,' she retracted incoherently, 'because you said you loved me and that means however stupid I've been you still love me. I…' She was crying once more but managed to sob, 'I'm going to the cottage again. I'm staying there. I don't want to leave. I—'

The beep told her her time was up and she stared at the phone stupidly before putting it down. Had she told him she loved him? She couldn't remember now. Had she? She must have done. She had been going to say it when she'd been cut off but she must have said it before, surely? Or perhaps not.

She surprised Harvey by stamping her foot, the tears streaming down her face. She couldn't even make a telephone call. How could she hope to put

things right when she couldn't even make a telephone call? She would call him again tomorrow.
She would keep on calling until he talked to her.

Ten minutes later she and Harvey were in the
car, heading away from London. The twilight
shadows were thick now but it wasn't completely
dark, although it would be by the time she arrived.
She couldn't wait to get to the cottage. She had
felt totally at odds from the second she'd arrived
back in the city. It had been as though she had
always lived in the tranquil surroundings of
Shropshire rather than the other way round. The
traffic noise, the dust, the heat, had seemed over-
whelming, even the things she'd always loved—
the hustle and bustle of cosmopolitan life, the
shops, the entertainment—had held no appeal.
Nothing had held any appeal. But then it wouldn't
without Travis.

The cottage was wonderfully familiar when
Beth finally nosed the car into the front garden
after opening the big swing gate. She felt as if she
had come home. Blinking back the tears, she let
an ecstatic Harvey out of the car and retrieved the
key from under the plant pot, lugging in her bags
and cases as Harvey began a thorough inspection
of the lawn and flowerbeds. She had just put the
last items away in the fridge when Harvey began
a frenzied barking.

Travis? She rushed to the front door but, on opening it, saw Harvey was in a corner of the lawn, nosing at something and then leaping back before trying again, barking all the time and totally ignoring her when she called his name.

It had to be one of the resident hedgehogs. Harvey had had run-ins with them before, which always resulted in the hedgehogs ambling off scot free and smug and Harvey with a pricked and sore nose. She didn't fancy another visit to the local vet tomorrow for antibiotics and goodness knew what.

Yelling did no good, so after finding her shoes, which she'd kicked off minutes before, Beth ran across the lawn. She was halfway when awful reality dawned. Stopping dead, she turned. The door was shut. The key was inside. The car was locked. Instinct had made her pull the door to behind her and the latch had clicked. She had done it again.

She checked the door but she knew it was useless. It didn't budge an inch.

For a second Beth didn't know whether to laugh or cry. In the event she did neither. After lugging Harvey away from the disdainful hedgehog, she sat down on the step and considered her options. It didn't take long.

It was just past midnight on a Friday night. A warm, moonlit summer's night, admittedly, but it would still get a mite chilly in the early hours and she wasn't even wearing a cardigan over the vest top and combat trousers she'd changed into for the drive from London. She could either sit it out through the hours of darkness and then trudge the few miles to the village in the morning, or walk to Travis's house right now and see if he was up for the weekend. Throw herself on his mercy—again.

A couple of minutes later she and Harvey were carefully picking their way along the lane, or at least she was. Harvey was prancing about like something demented, beside himself with excitement at the unexpected bonus of a midnight walk.

Beth tried not to think about what she would say to Travis if he was at home. This was made easier by the fact she was having to concentrate very hard on not stumbling in the darkness; the trees bordering the lane formed a canopy overhead which was very picturesque in daylight but made the lane almost pitch-black compared with the moonlit night beyond it.

Eventually the gates were in front of her—she'd arrived. And, toe-curlingly, there were lights downstairs and two vehicles on the drive. *Two?* Beth peered at them from the gate. The Mercedes Estate and a Range Rover. Travis had a visitor. Her stomach did such a flip she involuntarily put her hands on it. It didn't have to be a woman. She shut her eyes tightly before opening them wide. The urge to turn tail and walk away was strong. Truth time, she told herself silently. Do you believe in him or not?

Flooded by emotions as chaotic as a stormy sea, Beth walked up the pebbled drive to the large horseshoe-shaped area directly in front of the house where the cars were parked. Harvey had raced ahead, delighted with where they had finished up. Sheba and Sky lived here so it had to be good.

She stood, her heart racing, for some moments before she rang the bell. Then she waited. Harvey had sat down expectantly at her feet, his eyes trained on the front door. In other circumstances the earnestness in his stance would have made her smile.

She heard Travis's deep voice call something to someone inside the house the moment before he opened the door, which gave her a second's warning. Then she was staring into his face, his dear, dear face. And he was staring at her, blankly. As though he didn't know who she was. Or as though he didn't want to know who she was? Had he decided to wash his hands of her?

Gathering every ounce of courage, Beth said huskily, 'Hello, Travis.' And then she waited.

The blank expression vanished, his voice strangled as he said, 'Beth. I wasn't sure if my mind

was playing tricks. I thought you were in London.'
He stared at her, his eyes narrowing.

Harvey had pushed his way into the house,
careless of whether he was welcome or not, and
a moment later a female voice called, 'Travis?
There's another dog in here.'

'You've got company.'

Beth wasn't aware her face had drained of
colour but now his hand came out to take her
wrist, his voice more normal as he said, 'It's my
vet,' before calling, 'Harvey, come here.' Harvey
appeared instantly but only so far as Travis's side.
Bending and taking his collar, Travis said, 'I'll put
him with Sheba in my study,' and he pulled her
into the hall before shutting the door. 'Stay there.
Don't move. I'll be back.'

Beth stood exactly where she was as Travis led
Harvey to his study, her brain trying to compute
through the shock which had frozen it when she
heard a woman's voice. She had thought… She
shook her head. Travis was walking back to her
and he finished the thought as he said, 'You
thought I had a woman here?'

The words were one thing, the question behind
them was another. She stared at him. She had to
handle this right. The woman was a vet, which
meant something was the matter with Sky. 'You
have,' she said steadily. 'What is wrong?'

'You thought I had a date?' he persisted, watching her closely.

Travis being Travis, he wasn't about to be deflected. 'Only for a moment.' She wasn't about to lie. She would never lie to Travis again. 'When you didn't return my phone call and then, hearing a female voice, what was I supposed to think? I... I sent you away. I wouldn't have blamed you if you'd had a date here. You would have had every right, I know that.'

'Phone call?' His brow had wrinkled but the piercing grey eyes were burning into hers. 'What phone call?'

'I phoned your mobile earlier.'

'It's probably in the car.' She watched him take a deep breath. 'Why did you call?' he asked softly.

'To tell you I lied to you. I love you. I have done for a long time but I was too frightened to admit it—'

Her words were cut off by his mouth on hers and his arms wrapping themselves round her, whereupon he lifted her right off her feet. His mouth was hungry, bruising, but she didn't mind. She had thought she would have to plead and beg and persuade him to listen to her but it had only taken three words in essence. Three words she should have said days ago. She clung to him, kissing him back with all her heart and feeling giddy with relief and a soaring love that was spiralling higher and higher until she felt faint with the wonder of it.

'Travis?' His name came from beyond the world that was the two of them.

It was a moment before the voice penetrated their hunger and need of each other, and then he lifted his mouth from hers, setting her on her feet as he said distractedly, 'It's Sky, I have to help…'

'I'll come,' Beth said breathlessly. To the ends of the earth.

She didn't know what to expect as she followed Travis into the kitchen, but it wasn't the sight of Sky lying in a huge basket with four tiny scrambling puppies in a towel-lined box at the side of her. They were making soft mewing noises.

The vet, an attractive middle-aged woman whom Beth thought she recognised vaguely from the veterinary practice she had visited for Harvey's hedgehog abrasions, looked up as they entered and she was smiling. 'Last one's just popped out now. The problem was the big boy who came first; he was acting like a cork. Once he was out she had no difficult with his sisters.'

'Oh, they're gorgeous.' Beth gazed entranced at the sight. 'You didn't tell me,' she added softly to Travis.

'He didn't know.' The vet grinned at her. 'I got a frantic call earlier to say Sky seemed to be in a great deal of pain and acting strangely. It was a relief to find she was whelping.'

'It's all that fur.' For the first time since she had known him, Travis was embarrassed. 'They're both like great bears; now, aren't they?' He appealed to both women. 'I thought she was getting fatter but they both eat like horses anyway.'

'Bears, horses…' The vet was laughing as she rose to her feet, flexing her back. 'Well, Travis, you've got an addition of four healthy pups to the family. Who's the lucky father? Do I know him, by any chance?'

Travis looked at Beth. And then he smiled.

For a minute she didn't understand. Then, her hand going to her mouth, she murmured, 'He isn't? Not Harvey?'

'Only male they've been in contact with for months.' Travis grinned. 'I thought he was looking pleased with himself on occasion. I just hope Sheba is still chaste and virtuous. Hell.' There was a real note of panic in his voice. 'I've just shut Harvey in with her.'

'I'll check her if you like before I go,' the vet offered.

A couple of minutes later she was back. 'Don't worry about shutting the dog in with her tonight,' she said cheerfully. 'The job was done some time ago. I think the events of tonight will be repeated in roughly three weeks.'

Travis shut his eyes for an infinitesimal moment.

Beth stood watching the puppies, who were now snuggled in the basket with mum and suckling, while Travis showed the vet out. When he walked back into the kitchen she said immediately, 'I'm so sorry, Travis, about Harvey. All these puppies…'

'Force of nature.' He took her in his arms, stroking her face and stopping more words with his lips. When he raised his mouth from hers a little while later she was trembling and aching. 'Say it again,' he whispered against her lips. 'Tell me you love me. I've been waiting a lifetime to hear it.'

'I love you,' she breathed, the puppies snuffling at their feet. 'I love you more than I had dreamed it was possible to love.'

'And trust?' His hand tilted her chin so she was looking directly into the deep pools of his eyes. 'What about trust?'

'That too. I promise you, that too.'

She had expected something of an interrogation but again he accepted what she said without hesitation. Because *he* trusted her, Beth thought humbly. Loved and trusted *her.* John Turner was right, Travis was a good man. A giant among men, a man she wanted to be beside for the rest of her life. Suddenly all the things she had thought were lost for ever—a home shared with the man she loved, children, togetherness—were in front of her again and it was heady.

'You are the love of my life, Beth.' His voice was very quiet but there was a quality to it which brought tears to her eyes. 'If you'll let me, I want to spend the rest of my life proving it to you. Will you marry me?'

For a second, just the tiniest second, the enormity of what she was doing swept over her. Then she looked into his steady grey eyes, which were shining with such a love she felt like a queen before it. 'Yes,' she said, her eyes shining. 'Oh, yes, Travis. Yes, yes, yes!'

Beth didn't want a big wedding, just family and a few close friends like Mavis and Dave and their children. They agreed they would throw a huge party for everyone else when they came back from their honeymoon.

They were married in the little parish church in Shropshire two months after Travis proposed, on a mild sunny early October afternoon. Afterwards everyone piled back to the house where Travis had had a marquee erected in the garden. It was wonderfully informal, children running about laughing and playing and the adults sitting talking or dancing to the small band Travis had hired. The champagne flowed, folk ate when they felt like it from the delicious buffet and everyone congratulated Travis on having such an exquisitely lovely bride.

It didn't escape Beth's attention that all the women present—even the happily married ones—couldn't keep their eyes off Travis either. His rugged good looks lent a faintly brooding Heathcliff air to the formal wedding finery which was thrillingly romantic. But Beth didn't mind them looking. Travis was hers, always and for ever. She was completely sure about that now.

The puppies, all nine of them in various sizes—four from Sky and another five from Sheba—were the hit of the day with the children. Harvey strutted around as though he was a sultan with a harem, which she supposed he was in a way, Beth thought fondly. Even the two puppies she and Travis had chosen to keep were females. The other seven they'd found good homes for, Catherine and Michael having earmarked Sky's enormous firstborn whom Catherine declared was the very image of his handsome father.

'You're the most beautiful bride in the world; everyone's said so,' Travis whispered in Beth's ear later that evening as they danced to a slow romantic number the band was playing. It was true. Beth's Duchesse ivory silk dress was deceptively simple, but the way the close-fitting gown emphasised her tiny waist and perfect figure made it breathtaking. Instead of a veil, a profusion of tiny pink rosebuds were threaded through her upswept hair, the same flowers reflected in the posy she carried.

The look on Travis's face as he had turned to see her walk up the aisle had reduced all the women present in the church to tears even before the service had started.

Beth reached up and nuzzled her lips in the deliciously fragrant hollow under his ear, wanting him so badly she ached with it. As always he read her mind. 'When do you think they'll all go home?' he murmured, his body providing ample proof he was as aroused as she was. 'Soon? Very soon?'

Beth giggled. 'Not for ages. Everyone's enjoying themselves too much. I think they're here for the duration!'

'Then we'll have to make our goodbyes and leave them to it.'

'We can't.' Beth was genuinely shocked. "What will people think?'

'That I can't wait to have you to myself and they're damn right,' Travis answered drily. 'Come on, we're leaving.'

Sandra and Travis's mother—his stepfather had excused himself from attending the wedding due to pressure of business, much to everyone's unspoken relief—were staying at the house taking care of all the dogs until they returned from honeymooning in Italy. Travis had reserved the honeymoon suite at a local hotel from where they would go straight to Italy the next morning. Now he took her hand, kissing the palm in such a way her legs turned to jelly. 'All right,' Beth whispered. This would be their first time together and she wanted him as much as he wanted her. Other people faded into insignificance.

The night the puppies had been born she had shyly offered to accompany him to the master bedroom, but he had taken her hands, holding her slightly away from him, as he'd said, 'Thank you for your love and trust in me, my darling, and I want you more than words can say, but we're going to do this right. I won't pretend I haven't had women, Beth, but you know that. But you're different, *this* is different. The rest of your life starts now and it's going to start right. I want you for my wife, the mother of my children, and that sets you apart. Do you understand what I'm saying? You are worth waiting for.'

She had nodded, faintly bewildered nonetheless.

'Having said that, my nobility only goes so far,' Travis had continued wryly. 'This will be a short engagement, OK? A very short engagement.'

They drove away from the house in a shower of rice and confetti, Sandra having caught the bouquet Beth threw from the taxi cab. They sat close together in the back of the car, their hands entwined. The evening shadows were long and a soft scented darkness enveloped the world outside the cab but Beth was conscious only of her husband and what he meant to her. Which was everything—her sun, moon and stars.

Travis had said this was the start of the rest of their lives and she believed that. All that had gone before—Keith, her first marriage, the disaster it had become—was in the past. The future was theirs, to make of it what they would, and she intended it would be good. Very good.

When they stepped out of the taxi cab the fragrance of woodsmoke was lazy in the warm autumn air; the sky was velvet, pierced with stars and flooded with pale moonlight. A sense of whispering stillness pervaded the perfect night, timeless and enchanting as the sound of the car faded away.

Travis stood with his arm round her waist, his head lifted to the harvest moon. 'There will be other nights like this,' he murmured huskily as the silence of the night enfolded them. 'A lifetime of them. And one day when the children have grown up and gone and it's just the two of us again, I'll remind you of tonight. I'll tell you how beautiful you are and how much I love you, what a lucky man I am.'

'And I'll tell you you saved me,' Beth whispered back, touching his chiselled face with the palm of her hand. 'And that I love you more than life itself.'

The honeymoon suite was sumptuous and modern in shades of cream and gold, champagne on ice and a huge basket of strawberries waiting for them. Travis and Beth saw nothing but each other.

He undressed her slowly, relishing every long-awaited moment and she rewarded him with total surrender. As her dress fell to the floor, she stepped out of it, reaching for him and glorying in the expression on his face. "I want you to make love to me,' she told him very seriously. 'I've wanted it from the first time we met.'

Travis smiled slowly. 'Why the hell has it taken us so long when we've been of the same mind?' he drawled softly.

In the briefest moment of time the world faded away and they let their bodies speak for them, seeking each other greedily. Travis ripped off his own clothes, Beth's fingers clumsy and feverish as she helped him, and then they were both naked, taking in the scent and feel of each other as they swayed together in the middle of the opulent room.

Letting her body speak for her, Beth moved her hips against his, her breath coming in gasps as his mouth trailed from her throat to the rounded fullness of her breasts. He was already hugely aroused but the amazing control she had sensed more than once held, his mind and body alert as he nipped and caressed and tasted her until she lost the last remnants of restraint.

Drawing her over to the huge bed, he urged her down among the scented sheets and pillows and continued the sensual onslaught, murmuring such words of love and passion that she didn't try to hide the fulfilment she so desperately wanted. But still he didn't take her, kissing every part of her and creating such a raw and primitive need that her legs wrapped round his, fracturing the last shred of his constraint.

She gasped as he entered her, her nails digging into his shoulderblades and her breathing fast and wild. She hadn't thought such intensity of pleasure could exist but then the fierce rhythms within the core of her became all-consuming and he took her to a place she had never been before, a place where there was only the two of them and the rest of the world ceased to exist.

It felt like a long time before she could move or even open her eyes, but when she did the grey gaze was waiting for her. 'Well, Mrs. Black?' He traced a path down the side of her face with a lazy finger. 'Worth waiting for?'

She touched her fingers to his mouth, her voice

holding wonder and bewilderment. 'I never knew,' she whispered faintly. 'I've never before…'

He smiled. 'It's the jackpot, sweetheart,' he murmured throatily. 'Heaven on earth. It's what happens when you're one part of a perfect whole.'

'Did you know? That it could be so…'

'If you're asking me if I've ever come close to feeling like this then the answer's no.' He pulled her against him, the slow heavy beat of his heart and the rough feel of his body hair against the smooth silkiness of her skin intoxicating. 'You've blown me away, woman, if you want to know. You were everything I've ever dreamed of, every fantasy I've ever had. My perfect, beautiful, amazing Beth.' He took her face in his strong hands, cupping it tenderly as he kissed her long and deeply on the lips. 'For ever,' he whispered against the hot flushed skin of her face. 'Does that bother you? Frighten you? Even just the slightest? You can tell me, I won't mind.'

'Of course it doesn't.' The love in her eyes was answer enough for him.

'All the gremlins vanquished?' he said, his smile growing.

'They didn't stand a chance once I'd met you.'

'I'm going to make up for every minute of un-happiness you've ever had, every blue mood, every tear you've cried.' Suddenly the amusement had gone and he was deadly serious, his hand tracing her face with exquisite gentleness. 'I can't change the past, my darling, but I can make the future ours and it will be wonderful.'

She wondered if he'd guessed she'd shed a tear for her mother that morning, aching for her to see her dressed in her wedding finery. She thought so. He seemed so tender.

'We're going to be more happy than any couple has ever been since the foundation of the world, do you believe that?' he murmured against her lips. 'Do you feel it deep inside?'

She nodded. His hands were working their magic again and she was finding speech impossible.

His arms tightened around her and, as she met him kiss for kiss, she wondered what she had ever done to deserve such a love as this. As her body melted into his, she knew she wanted nothing more for the rest of her life than this man beside her.

Much later they fell asleep in each other's arms, entwined and fitted together like a perfect living jigsaw, replete and content. Two lives joined together for eternity, two hearts beating as one. Despite all the odds, they had found each other— the dream had become reality. They were home.

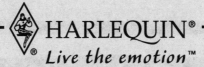

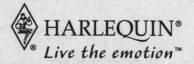

HARLEQUIN®
INTRIGUE®

BREATHTAKING ROMANTIC SUSPENSE

Shared dangers and passions lead to electrifying romance and heart-stopping suspense!

Every month, you'll meet six new heroes who are guaranteed to make your spine tingle and your pulse pound. With them you'll enter into the exciting world of Harlequin Intrigue— where your life is on the line and so is your heart!

THAT'S INTRIGUE—
ROMANTIC SUSPENSE
AT ITS BEST!

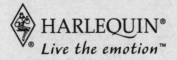

HARLEQUIN®
Presents®

The world's bestselling romance series...
The series that brings you your favorite authors,
month after month:

Helen Bianchin...Emma Darcy
Lynne Graham...Penny Jordan
Miranda Lee...Sandra Marton
Anne Mather...Carole Mortimer
Susan Napier...Michelle Reid

and many more uniquely talented authors!

Wealthy, powerful, gorgeous men...
Women who have feelings just like your own...
The stories you love, set in exotic, glamorous locations...

Seduction and Passion Guaranteed!

HARLEQUIN®

Super Romance®

…there's more to the story!

Superromance.
A *big* satisfying read about unforgettable
characters. Each month we offer *six* very different
stories that range from family drama to adventure
and mystery, from highly emotional stories to
romantic comedies—and much more! Stories
about people you'll believe in and care about.
Stories too compelling to put down….

Our authors are among today's *best* romance
writers. You'll find familiar names and talented
newcomers. Many of them are award winners—
and you'll see why!

If you want the biggest and best
in romance fiction, you'll get it
from Superromance!

Exciting, Emotional, Unexpected…

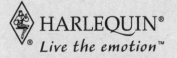

HARLEQUIN®
Live the emotion™